Bliss could eat no more. The odd note in her pocket and Colin's words combined to accuse her. More than that, she was trying to understand her reaction to his taking her hand while they had been in the living room. She couldn't believe the wave of feeling that had suddenly engulfed her. The unconscious, which she had tried to understand in others and control in herself, had suddenly overwhelmed her. She had wished for a moment that she was Polly, and that Colin would take her in his arms as he had her mother in their scene from *Private Lives*. Such a tumult of emotion had been unleashed in that moment as she had not experienced in an entire day with Howard Oaks. She hadn't asked for these feelings. She didn't want them. Not for Colin. Colin was dangerous. He made her feel like a liar and a hypocrite. She could do something about that.

SHEILA GREENWALD is the author and illustrator of many young adult books, including *It All Began with* Jane Eyre (available in a Dell Laurel-Leaf edition). Ms. Greenwald lives in New York.

Blissful Joy and the SATs

A Multiple-Choice Romance

by Sheila Greenwald

LAUREL-LEAF BOOKS bring together under a single imprint outstanding works of fiction and nonfiction particulary suitable for young adult readers, both in and out of the classroom. Charles F. Reasoner, Professor Emeritus of Children's Literature and Reading, New York University, is consultant to this series.

Published by
Dell Publishing Co., Inc.
1 Dag Hammarskjold Plaza
New York, New York 10017

Sample questions on pp. 25–26 reprinted by permission of Barron's Educational Series Inc. © copyright 1978. From Barron's *How to Prepare for College Entrance Examinations SAT* (9th edition) by Brownstein and Weiner.

Laurel-Leaf Library ® TM 766734, Dell Publishing Co., Inc.
YOUNG LOVE ® is a trademark of DC COMICS INC.

ISBN: 0-440-90481-1

RL: 5.7

Reprinted by arrangement with
Little, Brown and Company
Printed in the United States of America
First Laurel-Leaf printing—August 1983

To the memory of my grandparents
Lillian and Herman Friedman

Blissful Joy and the SATs

1

"*The only thing I can tell you about it,*" said the woman on the subway, of the filthy black dog at her feet, "*is it got on at Eighty-sixth Street.*"

Bliss Bowman, whose question the woman had just answered, shoved her SAT review book into her knapsack. "I never saw a dog on the subway before," she said.

"There's a first time for everything," the woman muttered darkly. "I never talk to strangers." She gathered her two worn shopping bags stuffed with empty Coca-Cola cans and rags, stood up, threw a piece of bagel to the dog, said, "My advice to you is don't get involved," and hurried from the car.

The advice came too late.

Bliss opened her book again and tried to concentrate on the page. She had always prided herself on her ability to surmount whatever distractions surrounded her. At that very moment she was completely ignoring a group of classmates who sat talking loudly only a few seats away.

"Harvard actually called Nora Lather? Are you kidding?"

"She got seven hundred eighty on her SATs, m'dear, and she's a basketball star."

"I heard she got six fifty and is a basket case."

"Six fifty isn't so bad."

"I thought it was six fifty combined."

"Eeeeek! Disney World Junior College, here she comes."

"Oh shut up. You with your seven hundred and twenty in math."

"I couldn't believe my score. I thought I really screwed up."

"Not like some people."

"Who?"

"You'd be surprised. A couple of the class brains."

"We've got class brains?"

"You know we do."

"Can this be?"

Bliss, who had been trying so hard not to listen that she was suffering ear strain, could not tell if they had spoken her name. Can *this* be? or, Can *Bliss* be? This or Bliss?

Susu Bennet and Francesca Stanhope got up to leave the car. They waved. "Bye, Bliss, congratulations on the science test," Susu called.

Bliss nodded.

"So long, Bowman," Francesca said without turning.

The rest of the group left at the next station. When they were all gone, Bliss closed her book. Well practiced though she may have been in ignoring school gossip, the little dog's steadfast gaze was quite another matter. She and the dog exchanged a long probing stare. One set of eyes dark, dumb-animal opaque, and drenched with emotion. The other cool, gray, intelligent, and guarded.

When she rose to leave the car at Christopher Street, the dog followed. It bustled along at her heels, through the turnstile and up the stairs to the street. It seemed to Bliss that an invisible leash, as strong as chain or leather, linked the dog to her. She could almost feel the pull of sympathy that joined them, hand to collar, eye to eye. The dog's gaze, worried, intense, and loving, followed her every movement.

Snow had begun to fall from a pewter March sky. Shopkeepers had salted their sidewalks. The black dog began to limp. First it held up one paw, then the other, pausing only to step into the gutter where it squatted, daintily yellowing and melting a patch of snow. The eyes on Bliss seemed to say, "I am a curb-trained female, intelligent and civilized." She did not lose pace again but turned exactly as Bliss did, bobbing up the stone steps of the building where Bliss lived, waiting on three paws till the outside door would be opened, then slipping through it with something of a flourish. They mounted the inside flights in unison. It wasn't until Bliss had let them both into the dark empty apartment that she spoke. "You can't stay here. In eighteen months I will be going to college out of town. I don't know what college, but I know the town won't be New York."

The large SAT review book unbalanced her bag so that it toppled off the hall bench. As she knelt to pick it up, the black dog bounded to her, put its face to her face and its tongue in her nose. She fell back on her heels. "Hey, cut that out. I said no deal. A dog has got to be walked and fed and cared for. Responsibility. You want to blackball my future plans?"

The dog drew back and sat perfectly still, as if too full of feeling to risk movement. Bliss stood up. "All right. As long as you're here, come on in." Together they went into

3

a small, cluttered kitchen. A square Formica table had not been cleared of breakfast crumbs and coffee mugs. There was a note propped up against an open jam jar. Bliss read it out loud. "Aft wrk may flick out. Chpd Bf in Frg, froz pots too. Heat 'n Eat. Ciao, cara mia."

"Ciao yourself, Cara Mama," Bliss said to the note. "My mother the escape artist." She sponged off the table, put the dishes in the sink, and filled a bowl of water for the dog. The telephone rang.

"Blissy."

"Jenny, you won't believe what has followed me home."

"Multiple choice? Analogies or antonyms?"

"Analogies, multiple choice. '*Bliss* is to *followed* as . . .'"

"Beautiful stranger is to pursued."

"Little black dog is to tailed."

"Little black dog? How do you spell that tail? Are you serious?"

"I am about to tell it to go to the ASPCA. As soon as it finishes its food and water."

"Don't give it food and water. You'll get involved."

"That's what the bag lady said."

"What bag lady?"

"The one on the subway who told me it got on at Eighty-sixth Street. Why does everyone say, 'Don't get involved,' as if getting involved were neurotic?"

"*You're* the one who told *me* that."

"Yes, I did," Bliss admitted.

"You know yourself, as an only child you are subconsciously in search of a substitute sibling. Being the victim of divorce intensifies the problem. Also I detect a touch of separation anxiety. The conscious Bliss is saying she wants to go to Vassar, but the subconscious Bliss is looking for an excuse to stay home and be a baby."

"I thought of all that," Bliss lied. "Now I have to go change my diaper." She hung up.

"That was Jenny Sewel," Bliss told the dog. "She is my best, and also my only, friend. She disapproves of you. So do I."

The dog had finished a bowl of water as well as a cup of Bran Chex.

"You're filthy; I'd better wash you up before I take you in. You'll have a better chance of getting adopted if you're clean."

As the tub was filling, Bliss removed a cracked collar with no tags from around the animal's neck. "I need to call you something." She lowered the dog into water and suds. "But I'll have to be careful. At the top of the list of things I hold against Polly and Dan is the name they gave me. Blissful Joy Bowman. Did you ever hear anything so doomed? I wouldn't do that to a dog." Rivulets of black water ran off the animal's back. Bliss emptied the tub and filled it again. Watching the water, her mind slipped without warning into what Jenny called a mental tick and Bliss called an SAT spasm. *If the water is flowing into the tub at the rate of a gallon every six minutes and is draining at a rate of a gallon every ten minutes, how much water does the tub contain after three minutes of flowing?* "Help." She yanked the faucet shut in an effort to rid herself of the spasm. There were two soapings and one rinsing before the water ran clean.

"At last," Bliss sighed. "You're beautiful." She drew back to admire the lustrous wet black coat she had certainly had a hand in creating. "Beautiful," she said again. "What am I doing talking out loud to a dumb animal? What's happening to me?" She stroked the wet springy head hairs. "I haven't been attached to anything since my

5

Raggedy Ann doll. Took her everywhere. Couldn't sleep without her. Of course she was stolen by one of the kids at the Creative Community Nursery School, creatively stolen, Dan said." As Bliss spoke, the dog appeared to be trying to follow her. With her head at a listening tilt, her intent brown gaze had pulled the painful tale out of Bliss's storehouse of unfortunate events, and at the same time had struck a well of affection that had not been tapped since the disappearance of the long-lost doll. "We'll buy you another doll," Polly and Dan had told her. "For heaven's sake stop carrying on. They sell them at every toy store."

But it had been *that* doll. She had told secrets to *that* doll. She had slept with, eaten with, and cared for *that* doll. That doll had waited for her when she came home from places, or had gone with her to new houses or schools to share her life. When that doll was gone, Bliss had decided not to let herself open to another hurt so large. There would be no more dolls. No more involvements (as she later learned to call them) that could lead to such misery. Life was hard enough without getting swamped with affections that could distort one's judgment and cause nothing but pain.

Bliss lifted the dog out of the tub, set her on a towel, and impulsively bent to kiss the glistening black head. Just as her lips touched the wet brow, the dog squared off for a shakedown that sprayed Bliss like a summer shower.

She fell back on her knees, laughing. "Was that supposed to be funny?"

"Blissy, are you in there alone, or what?" Polly rapped on the door.

"I'm 'or what.' "

Polly opened the door and leaned on its frame. "Good

grief, are you out of your skull?" Her ratty fur jacket and purple velour hat were dusted with melting snowflakes. Her face was pale and raw from cold. "You know you can't have a dawg."

Bliss sat on the edge of the tub. She reached down and rested her hand reassuringly on the animal's head. "It doesn't really concern you."

"Doesn't concern ME? They've got to be walked and fed and loved. They're a big responsibility. Like a kid."

"How would you know, Pol?"

"What are you giving me?"

"I'm keeping the dog." Bliss shrugged. "The subject is closed."

So was the door.

And that was how Bliss Bowman, who never wanted one, got a dog.

2

At sixteen and one-half Blissful Joy Bowman bore a chip on her shoulder large enough to have qualified as a small boulder. Aside from her name, her list of wrongs done to her by life included the fact that she had been born to a pair of childlike, unreliable, disorganized actors, who had never been able to get their act together enough to do more than sue for divorce. It struck Bliss that the divorce was the first project Polly and Dan had ever completed successfully. It even changed their luck from perfectly dreadful to bad.

On the plus side Bliss counted the fact that her parents were not unfriendly to one another and lived within walking distance. Both sets of grandparents were alive and well off enough to pick up the larger bills. Best of all Bliss had learned at an early age that since she could not depend upon Polly and Dan she had best find a careful, mature, unimpulsive person to rely on. Herself. She planned her life and left nothing to chance or luck. She attended an excellent school, was first in her class, would apply for early decision to Vassar College and be free of what Polly and Dan called their "casual life-style" and what she called their "mess."

So it was in something of a stunned silence that unimpulsive, plan-making, careful Bliss stared through the steamy vapors in the bathroom at the small beast she had just informed her mother was to be hers against every iota of good sense she possessed. "I think I will have to name you Blackball," she said.

"Why are you home so early?" Bliss asked Polly in the kitchen. "Your note said you'd be at the movies."

Polly was poking around in the refrigerator, pulling out plastic-wrapped leftovers in the frantic way she had of dealing with everything in the kitchen.

"My throat was scratchy and that office was just making me sick. It's the worst yet. I told the agency, I hate doctors' offices. Architects, decorators, designers, galleries, anything." She filled the kettle and set a light under it. "One cup of tea, hold the sympathy." Polly tugged on the sleeve of her tie-dyed thermal underwear and ran her long fingers through the great cloud of white-blond hair that frizzed out from her angular face. "I just wish I could get a soap. If I could get a soap, then I wouldn't have to sit in those squalid Plexiglass booths and answer the phone. 'Dr. Dumbo's Office.' Or a showcase. Maybe I can get into one of the Equity productions. Of course they don't pay, but they're great exposure. I could use that. All these classes at the Actors Lab should begin to pay off."

"You *do* look pale," Bliss said. "About the dog, Polly . . ."

"Oh forget it." Polly threw up her skinny arms. "I was just surprised, that's all. Everybody always said you should have a dog. *My* therapist, *Dan's* therapist, the school psychologist, your grandmother. All the books on single-parented only children, sob gulp boo hoo."

The kettle began to whistle. In the long-legged stride that was part of her style, Polly moved to the stove and poured water over a soggy tea bag left in a mug by the sink.

"The therapists said that about fourteen years ago," Bliss reminded her mother. "And I wish you would take responsibility for your own point of view, Pol. Instead of 'the therapist said, the psychologist said.' What do *you* say?"

"Here we go," Polly murmured to her mug. She sat down and turned large reproachful eyes on Bliss. "I should have called you Blister. Blister Bowman, raw, about to burst. No way I touch you is ever right."

"I am just trying to help you see some of the patterns of behavior that have crippled you, Polly."

"What do you charge? I mean where's your office? I mean when you hang up your shingle gimme a card. I'll send my friends. Till then would you keep your diagnoses to yourself? Right now I have all I can handle with the flu."

Bliss turned on her heel. She knew from long experience that it would be downhill between herself and Polly from now on. She had been analyzing Polly's mood swings for months (ever since reading a book on mood swings). She knew the pattern. Two hours of self-pity and depression, followed by a telephone call to a friend and a session at the record player listening to Ella Fitzgerald sing Gershwin or Rodgers and Hart, after which the clouds would part and a wan smile appear.

"Since you're leaving home," Polly called after her,

"would you go over to Shopwell and pick up some milk and salad stuff? We're out."

As she walked to the market, Bliss had to admit that Polly had stumbled on the truth. She did dream of one day "hanging out a shingle." Dr. B. J. Bowman, Ph.D. Psychology. She had seen the brass plaque in her fantasies. She had seen herself too. Cool, wise, confident, seated at a modern desk in a sun-filled office. She knew how she would look. Her grandmother, Ruth Prentice, was a practicing psychologist. Bliss practiced psychology too, whenever possible. She tried to identify and categorize the particular personality type, neuroses, or psychoses she encountered among the people she knew. This endeavor served two purposes. It helped prepare her for her chosen field and gain perspective on her own world, as well as give her a sense of confidence (even superiority). It helped to keep her at a distance from events that might hurt. She noted that the people upon whom she practiced often reacted with hostility and nerves. That was okay too.

In a small bound notebook she jotted down her more interesting observations.

> Polly Prentice. A bright, pretty, spoiled daughter of doting parents had been given everything her heart desired. Good looks, good grades, good voice, popularity, and the lead in every school play. Went to Vassar. Worked in summer stock and met Dan Bowman.

> Dan Bowman. A handsome, spoiled bright son of doting parents. Had been given everything his heart desired. Good looks, good grades, good voice, popularity, and the lead in every school play. Went

11

to Columbia. Worked in summer stock and met Polly Prentice.

Polly and Dan got married and came to New York to take the town by storm. Couldn't find work. Quit the theater to write a novel. Quit the novel to write a play. Quit the play to write for TV. Blissful Joy was born. Polly quit Dan. Dan quit Polly.

COULD THAT MARRIAGE HAVE BEEN SAVED?

We'll never know, because Polly met Trevor Frisch at the opening night party of her first off-Broadway job, and was head over heels trying to save her second marriage before she could have reflected on the first.

When she got to Shopwell, Bliss bought a red leash and a collar studded with nail heads, a box of dog chow and a chew stick, along with salad stuff and milk. She walked the two blocks home in a thick silent fall of wet flakes.

Polly and Dan, the bright, romantic, good-looking dreamers who thought life was a fairy tale out of the Disney Studio, in which any minute something fantastic and magical would happen, were a dime a dozen. But Bliss Bowman, sixteen and one-half, confronting her reality and her future with plans and purpose, was rare indeed. Bliss knew exactly where she was going. To a wonderful college, a fine graduate school, a professional career, and a NORMAL life.

In the meantime she was heading home happy and excited to see the dog she wouldn't give up for anything.

3

"I feel rotten," Polly whimpered from the living-room sofa. She balanced her mug of tea on her stomach. Her long legs were stretched the length of the cushions and Bliss's baby blanket was over her feet. On the floor beside the sofa and on the coffee table in front of the sofa were mounds of yellow legal pad papers on which Polly was currently writing her autobiography. Polly wrote away at it with a fervor that Bliss found ominous. Everything about this manuscript struck Bliss as bad for Polly, not to mention herself. For herself she minded the invasion of privacy; for Polly, the tendencies toward exhibitionism (groups of friends gathered to hear the latest chapter) and dreams of fame and glory. "When this book is published and I sell the paperback and movie rights for a fortune, I'll be able to tell Office Temporaries where to get off. I'll produce my own shows. I'll travel." Bliss knew these were the sorts of musings which set her mother up for disappointment and depression.

"I called Dan while you were out. I think you ought to go over to his place so you don't pick up whatever I've got."

"But can you manage?"

"It's only influenza," Polly rasped dramatically. "You certainly don't need it. I know how important school is now, what with those tests, the PSTUPIDs, coming up."

"It's the SATs. I had the PSATs. The P is for practice. Practice Standard Achievement Test. Don't worry. I'll have two cracks at the real thing."

"In my day we only had one," Polly sighed in happy recollection.

"I guess you were lucky."

"As it turned out, I was."

It was legendary in the Prentice family that Polly had received a perfect score in her College Board exam. She had been accepted by Radcliffe, Bryn Mawr, Vassar, and Barnard. Bliss could never get over it.

As if reading her thoughts, Polly said, "Just because I've been dumb at life doesn't mean I couldn't be smart in school, kiddo. When you grow up you find out subtle things, like one has nothing whatsoever to do with the other."

"Let's hope the score I got on the PSATs has nothing to do with the one I'll get on the SATs," said Bliss worriedly.

"You had a virus that day."

"And I was so nervous too."

"Why don't you go to one of those cram schools? It's not an admission of failure."

"You can't cram for an aptitude test. The pamphlet they send you explains that," Bliss said coldly. "I bought the review book. I'll work this out on my own. Don't pressure me."

14

"Please." Polly held up her hand and waved it like a white flag. "Stop reading things into what I say. I'm a sick woman."

Of course she read things into what Polly had said — that was, after all, her specialty. She knew that Polly was nearly hysterical over the low score she had gotten. Bliss herself could not fathom what had gone wrong. She thought she had done well. Polly's suggestion that she go to one of the cram schools had become an issue between them. Bliss had always handled school extremely well by herself. She had never needed a tutor or any outside help. She was the one who frequently helped classmates when they couldn't understand something. She would work at the Barron's review and master it. She had to. What would a college think of Blissful Joy Bowman who never got less than an A-minus for six years receiving a pitiful score on her SATs? She'd appear a fraud, an overachieving fake. The test, after all, judged INNATE APTITUDE.

Bliss collected her books and notes and stuffed some clean underwear into the spaces of her knapsack. She kept nightclothes and a toothbrush at Dan's. It was easier that way. Frequently Polly and Dan arranged at the last minute for Bliss to stay at her father's during the week. Dan and Polly, who had not been able to stay on speaking terms under one roof, could spend no end of time on the telephone. They called each other a few times a week to talk about Bliss and mutual friends, and to share information on casting calls. Bliss wondered: had they been able to speak on the phone instead of directly, might they have stayed married?

The snow had stopped. A few flakes fell, but the sky seemed to be clearing. The light was tentative, as if promising the longer dusks of spring. An inch or two of snow had been collected at the curb. Blackball marched like a

15

one-dog regiment at the end of her leash, looking up at Bliss from time to time for approval. Suddenly, without warning, she came to a dead stop. It was as if a rivet had gone through her. She lifted her head, sniffing, trembling, agitated, and lunged across the street, heading west.

"Hey, this isn't where we're going." Bliss tried to pull back, but the dog's energy carried her along in a mad dash. They flew across intersections full of heavy traffic, around corners, down winding side streets and finally came to a stop on a quiet afterthought of a village street, that curved between two large thoroughfares. The house before which the dog stood panting was an unrestored brownstone. Four steps down from the sidewalk was an areaway containing a tub full of dead-looking shrubs, a gate, and a red painted door. On the parlor floor Bliss was aware of a face at the window, but a shade snapped shut. The house, the street, the dead shrubs, the black iron gate, and blank front windows appeared threatening. She yanked on the leash and shivered. "Let's go."

4

By the time Dan Bowman backed into his own door, both arms laden with grocery bags, Blackball had found a spot on the carpet of his tiny bedroom and Bliss was half through her chemistry assignment, trying to distract herself from Blackball's upsetting detour to the house with the red door, and the vague notion that she had been followed the rest of the way to Dan's building by someone in a green jacket.

"Blissful Joy baby," Dan shouted, crashing the packages on the kitchen table and opening his long arms. "Hug time." After he had nearly fractured her nose on his collarbone, Dan held her off at arm's length for what Bliss called Daddy Dan's Drama. "Lovely child," he marveled in the voice he had been perfecting for the description of anything from liquid cleansers to paper towels on television commercials. "Ye Gods," she saw Blackball, "do we send it to college? Does it live in a dorm and major in Human Behavior?"

17

"I haven't thought that far ahead."

"Is this my Bliss? The long-range planner?" He cocked his head at her and hung up his coat. "We are having a guest for dinner. I took this opportunity to ingratiate myself with a lady."

"Oh Dan."

"I know, I didn't have to, but I couldn't resist. She is the vet from downstairs." He winked. "As soon as Polly called me with the news, 'Blisskins got a dawg,' I thought fast and rang my neighbor."

"Dan, you're impossible."

"What I had in mind were free rabies shots, toots." He emptied the grocery bags and tied an enormous apron with a stencil of Shakespeare's head on it around his waist. "Now to cook." Dan commenced to wash, chop, sauté, taste, and give orders. "Set the table. Use that Wedgewood of Grandma's and the Irish crystal. No, not those napkins. Mmmm, that smells divine. How's poor Polly? She sounded dreadful. Ouch, that thing's burning. I don't like your skirt. Where'd you get it? Looks like a Polly reject. From a let's-get-organized phase. Be an angel and fix me a bourbon."

Bliss set the table, fetched the bourbon, broke out the ice, and began to pour.

"I didn't say 'when.' Fill to the rim." Before long there were veal chops braising in wine, there was escarole steaming in oil and garlic, there were tiny potatoes browning in butter.

Watching her father, Bliss wondered if his outward disorganization concealed inner discipline, unlike Polly, whose outward disorganization mirrored inner chaos.

The doorbell rang. Blackball ran in a circle of anticipation. With his spoon in the air and a towel around his neck Dan ceremoniously bowed in a small woman carrying a bouquet of daffodils. She had a serious face in which every feature was long — long nose, long chin, and long brow. Her hair, however, was short, curly, and nearly gray. She held out the flowers and smiled indulgently at Dan, as if he were a remarkable child. When she smiled, her plain face was pleasant.

"My name is Delphi Pilpel," she told Bliss in slightly accented English. When she saw Blackball she sighed. "I suppose that's why you invited me. Ever since my husband died, friends have been pairing me up with their pets. I've been matched up with two Great Danes and a Labrador."

"How did it go?" said Dan.

"The Labrador was smitten. He had his head in my lap through the entire dinner. But when they brought him in for shots the next day, the romance was over."

"I think Blackball needs shots," said Bliss.

"I think I need my head in your lap," said Dan.

Doctor Pilpel laughed in a way that made Bliss uneasy. They all stood in the kitchen watching Dan finish cooking dinner.

"Pour out a glass of wine for yourself, Delphi," Dan said.

Bliss noticed that Doctor Pilpel's hand was trembling as she poured out the wine. The hand was long, but pale and beautifully shaped.

"Bliss found that dog on the subway," Dan said innocently. "Do you think she ought to be checked out?"

"She's an excellent Scottie," said Dr. Pilpel narrowing her eyes professionally at Blackball's torso. "I'm sure you called the police or the ASPCA to report that you found her."

Bliss looked down. "No. I didn't call anyone. I want to keep her."

"Bliss babes. I'll buy you another dog."

It was the same cheerful voice that had said, "Bliss babes, I'll buy you another Raggedy Ann." Never. "I want this dog."

"Sweetheart."

There was silence for some moments; the only sound was of the timer ticking and sizzling food.

"If you want to keep her," said Delphi Pilpel softly, "it is especially good that you make that call. Then if there's no report on her, you're done with it and can rest easy. If there is a report maybe you could work out something with the owner. Otherwise you will be in a state of limbo, wondering if one day somebody might recognize her and demand her return."

They took their wineglasses and went into what Dan called the dining-room-part-of-the-living-room. There was also the library-part-of-the-living-room and the guestroom-part-of-the-living-room. Dan lit the blue tapers in Grandma Bowman's second-best silver candlesticks and pulled out their chairs. The telephone rang. As her father went to answer the phone in the kitchen, Delphi Pilpel's admiring gaze followed him. "He moves so well," she said.

"He studied it."

Delphi blinked in the candlelight and sipped her wine.

"For you, Bliss." Dan returned to the table. "I'd have told her to call back after dinner, but she sounds desperate."

It was Sibyl Oaks and she was always desperate.

"Oh God, Bowman," she half sobbed. "I can't get the chemistry. It's like a block that's a blockade. Ratner says if I fail another test, I fail the semester."

"What do you want specifically?" Bliss asked. She

20

knew that Sibyl could circle a point for half an hour. "I'm in the middle of dinner."

"Can I call you later?"

"Not really." Bliss didn't want to miss a moment's observation of Dan and Delphi Pilpel. "Why don't I meet you before class tomorrow morning. Eight-fifteen in the Commons."

"You're saving my life."

Back in the dining-room-part-of-the-living-room, Dan was arranging the food artfully on his mother's second-best set of dishes. Delphi watched him, moonstruck. "You're not only a wonderful cook, but you make everything *look* so beautiful."

Dan smiled. "The arrangement is sort of Nouvelle Cuisine, don't you think?"

"I'm not used to this," she sighed and withdrew from her purse a pair of glasses with which to better admire her dinner. "I was never much of a cook and my husband had no interest in food. In fact, he literally had no stomach. We ate very bland things for his condition, and for me just the essentials."

"Purina and milk," said Dan, filling her glass with wine again.

She laughed. "Oh, I'm so glad you asked me up."

It struck Bliss that the wine had gone directly to Delphi's head. Her eyes were a bit swimmy and her features somewhat smudged. "I probably shouldn't say this," she said, wiping her mouth delicately with a linen napkin, "but I've been admiring you in the lobby for over a year."

"No, you shouldn't have said that," said Dan. "Bliss will tell you that one of my problems has been vanity and easy success with women."

Bliss nodded emphatically. "He trades on charm "

"What's wrong with that?" Delphi cried. "I wish I could do it. Instead I have to work so hard for everything. Here's to charm." She lifted her glass, which was nearly empty again.

Bliss was tempted to reach over, take her hand, and say, "STOP. He wants a rake-off on shots and office visits for my dog. You're not his type."

Dan told them about the commercial he had been working on that day. Hundreds of takes involving an instant coffee that was supposed to look richer. "Actually the spoon with the richer-looking coffee contained dirt."

"That's unethical," Bliss protested.

"What makes it ethical is the fact that they do not put dirt in your daddy's paycheck, Blissy. The coffee may not be richer, but I am."

Bliss observed Delphi Pilpel fall like Alice down the rabbit hole into love for charming Dan. She had seen it all before. However, this time instead of her usual attitude of detached amusement, she was sad. She liked Delphi Pilpel. She liked her funny long face and her graying hair and slightly crossed eye and uncapped teeth and the way she had of being so happy to have been asked. She knew for certain that Dan would never dream of any serious liaison with such a woman. Dan was a man for all seasons. Tonight was Dog Night. His taste ran to wood nymphs. Tall stringy girls, with fly-away hair and blown-away brains who quoted Neruda wrong, asked you what sign you were born under, burned the handles off the pots, let the tub overflow, and left when the weather changed.

Dan cleared the empty plates. Bliss reached down to pat Blackball, who had lain by her foot throughout dinner.

"If you don't locate her owner, bring her in for her shots and check-up," said Delphi. "She's really a good dog." She hiccuped and covered her mouth, embarrassed. "I don't know what's come over me."

"The wine maybe."

"Yes, perhaps. The wine and also I've had a very trying year. My husband's death, heaps of work. I'm all right during the day, but at night sometimes I get giddy." She looked suddenly earnest and upset. "Do you think I'm foolish?"

"No, no," Bliss assured her. "I like you."

"Do you suppose your father likes me?"

"Why wouldn't he?" She set her napkin on the table and stood up. "If you'll excuse me, I have to start my homework." She went into Dan's small bedroom to tackle the chemistry and plow through the nightly chapter in what Polly called the PSTUPID review book. Blackball jumped onto the bed and took possession of the pillow, her paws stretched its length. She gazed at Bliss, tipping her head to one side, her round emotional eyes wide, as if she were listening to her thoughts, trying to gauge them. Then her mouth opened in what looked incredibly like a smile and she lowered her chin onto the pillow. "We're safe, aren't we?" she seemed to acknowledge. "Warm and safe, lucky us." Her eyes remained on Bliss's face, watchful, loving, worried; this was no Raggedy Ann, but the most responsive creature on earth.

"I'll make a deal with you," Bliss whispered. "I'll call the ASPCA, but if they answer, I'll hang up." Instead she dialed Jenny Sewel. "I'm at my father's. You won't be able to guess what's going on."

"Multiple choice? Antonyms, analogies, or complete the sentence?"

23

"Multiple choice, complete the sentence. 'Dashing Dan is entertaining a lady veterinarian in order to dot dot dot dot.'"

"Obtain a cut rate for his daughter's new dog."

"That wins you a four-year scholarship to Oxford," Bliss said. "Furthermore, she's falling in love with him. Of course he has no interest in her at all. She is your classic insecure woman seeking the impossible rejecting male."

"Right out of a book I'm reading. *The Goldilocks Syndrome: Ten Case Histories of Self-Destructive Women*."

Jenny wanted to be a psychoanalyst. The two friends exchanged "case histories" often. Jenny was the adopted daughter of a social worker and a photographer. She was one-quarter American Indian, one-quarter Puerto Rican, one-quarter Vietnamese, and one-quarter black. "The private schools must have engineered my birth," she was fond of saying. "Four minority scholarships for the price of one."

"You know what a user Dan is. He wants free shots for my dog, in exchange for an evening's flirtation and a dinner. It's a good deal. The dinner costs no more than six dollars, including wine. Office visits would amount to over one hundred."

"But you're not keeping the dog."

"I am."

"Bliss, this is regression. Classic."

"There are all sorts of classics."

"Such as?"

"Rin Tin Tin. Lassie."

"Goldilocks," Jenny said bleakly.

When Bliss hung up she took a large calendar out from

the back pocket of her loose leaf and opened it. All the months of the year were spread before her on one page. The date May ninth stood out from the others by virtue of a circle around it in vermillion magic marker. Bliss unsheathed a black marker and crossed off the day that was concluding. March ninth. The X she slashed through March ninth joined the ones before it like the advance guard of an army of X's trudging relentlessly toward the red-circled May ninth, like troops toward Armageddon. May ninth, SAT. Beneath the X she had drawn over March ninth Bliss placed a small star-shaped squiggle to note the day on which she had found Blackball. Crossing off the day was the start of her nightly ritual. She sighed heavily and opened the thick Barron's review. Her eye rested on the introductory paragraph she had puzzled over many times. "The SATs tell the colleges how well you will perform."

Her heart sank. If this were true, why was it that she had "performed" so well in high school? Was there some mistake? She opened to the test, noted the time, and began. As usual the look of the page with its computer holes unnerved her. It was an exam for robots. Not touched by human hands, not made for human thought. A printout in computer-speak. An IBM brain probe for the space age. She set her teeth. *Filter: Water. A. Curtail: Activity. B. Expurgate: Book. C. Edit: Text. D. Condense: Novel. E. Censor: Play.* She bit the eraser of her number two pencil. Expurgate to book was a possibility, but she remembered so clearly the time Polly had volunteered to direct the spring play at her grade school and had to censor out the risqué lines. They had spent an afternoon going over all the scripts with a black pen inking out the lines that had to go as a filter would have removed offending sediment from water. She went on. *Benediction: Anathema. A. Marriage: Hatred. B. Eulogy: Vilification. C. Elegy: Lament. D. Elegy: Castigation. E. Maudlin: Sentimental.*

At this point her mind reeled. The words swam. She knew what they meant, she could use them in a sentence, she could explain them, but she could not deal with them as they were on the test. Shot at her as if by a firing squad, isolated, threatening, and unreal. After a few minutes of looking at them, they lost all meaning. Her eyes dimmed with nerves and hopelessness. She filled in the empty circles. She knew she was guessing blind, taking too long and finally out of time.

Checking her answers she found that *Censor: Play* was incorrect. *Expurgate: Book* was the right answer. She had been deluded by her own recollections, by her personal storehouse of associations. Would they always be there ready to leap out at her from dark corners of her mind to thwart her hopes for a future she had worked so hard to achieve? She had scored poorly. She got into bed. Blackball pressed her warm furry back against Bliss's stomach. They snuggled. She could hear Dan's and Delphi's voices muffled through the door. He would sleep in the guest-room-part-of-the-living-room. She reached out and turned off the bedside light. Blackball resettled herself and began to snore. "You are to affection," Bliss whispered into the dog's ear, "as the SATs are to misery."

5

As soon as she saw Sibyl Oaks waiting for her in the Commons, Bliss knew it was not going to be a good day. Sibyl's small heart-shaped face was cupped in one hand. In the other she held a paper carton of steaming black coffee. On every finger of that hand but the thumb, she wore a ring of the thinnest gold. Her bitten nails were enameled brown.

"I've tried everything," she said. "I set the dumb formulas to Gilbert and Sullivan. You can learn any gibberish that way, but this time it didn't work. Help." She sang a tune from *The Pirates of Penzance*, stumbling over the new lyrics which seemed to be a mishmash of chemical formulas.

Bliss sighed. Sibyl Oaks's case had been described to a T in an article Jenny had read her on adolescent schizophrenia and anorexia nervosa. Sibyl was thin as a rail, unable to tell the truth, and self-destructive. She did everything at the last minute, devising ingenious tricks to ram subject matter into her brain for the purpose of an exam. She was always late, frantic, on the verge of crises, expulsion, or probation. She told outrageous stories that no one believed and that she either forgot or contradicted. On the subject of pot: "I smoked it once in my life and it was contaminated. My lungs are shot forever." On the subject of sex: "I did it once in my life. The guy had V.D. My womb is shot forever." She had no friends.

The school Bliss attended had been started by a Miss Partridge and a Miss Mellon in the latter part of the nineteenth century for the daughters of the wealthy. The school was now called Partridge Mellon (the Misses having been dropped) but it was still all girls, and they were still by and large the daughters of the wealthy. However with a nod to changing times, outsiders like Jenny Sewel and Bliss Bowman had been granted admission. Bliss and Jenny often joked that they more than earned their half scholarships by giving PM juniors a soothing sense of mingling with the poor and disadvantaged. The definition of poverty and disadvantage being the need to survive without a housekeeper and a country estate. When on rare occasion Bliss and Jenny were invited to the house of a classmate, it was with the unspoken understanding that the visit would not be returned. This condescension didn't bother Bliss. She was getting what she wanted, a fine education at a prestigious school. One day she would wave them all good-bye without a backward glance.

Bliss and Sibyl opened their books. "I am the very model of a water soluble molecule," Sibyl sang to the Gilbert and Sullivan tune. "My trouble is I don't know enough to know what gibberish we're supposed to know."

Bliss looked down her page of notes. "She's certain to ask us the number of atoms in a mole."

"Oh Lord." Sibyl closed her eyes. "What sort of mole? Something on the cheek, or a furry little rodent? Help help. Tell me the answer quick."

"Six point zero times ten to the twenty-third."

Sibyl opened her eyes and tapped her fingers on the table, smiling. She began to sing to the tune of a toothpaste commercial "S-i-i-i-x point zero times tentada twenny-third are the atoms in a mole, whatta mole, guys, are the atoms in a mole."

Bliss snapped her book shut. "If you put some effort into learning this stuff instead of into making it nonsense, you'd get someplace."

"It *is* nonsense," said Sibyl with passion. "If I keep it nonsense, I'll pass. If I think about it, I'll fail. Don't ask me to think about it. My advice to you is, pick out one or two things in life to think about and reduce the rest of it to nonsense."

"You're hopeless."

"Listen Bowman, I won't ask you how you did on the PSATs, but I'll tell you how I did. Nearly perfect. You know why? Because it's a crock, and I treat it that way. Any time in my life I cared about a subject, I nearly flunked it." She looked so intense that Bliss believed her.

"I thought you were going to tell me that you took the SATs once, and they were contaminated, and now your brains are shot forever."

Sibyl tipped her chair back and roared. "Say, will you come home with me today?"

"I can't. I have to take my dog to the vet."

"Well, some other time. I know that except for Sewel you never visit, and I never invite. We'll be on a voyage of discovery."

They drilled each other in the chemistry until the bell rang for the start of classes.

"Thanks, Bowman." Sibyl gathered her frayed, split, splotched notebooks. "If I can ever help you to reduce this stuff to gibberish, let me know. I may save *your* life one day."

All through the exam, Bliss heard someone humming tunes from *The Pirates of Penzance*.

In Doctor Pilpel's waiting room there were five dogs and one man. He was reading a script. When Bliss walked past him, stepping over his dogs to take a seat on the catercornered leather sofa, he lifted his eyes just enough to see Blackball. "Oh halloo," he cried happily and raised his gaze, full of expectation, to Bliss. He started and frowned. "Sorry, I thought from the dog you'd be some-one else."

Bliss sat in the farthest corner of the sofa. But Black-ball pulled toward the man, wagging her tail as if at an old friend.

"There, there," he patted her head. She seemed to grow even more agitated. "I thought I knew the dog, you see," he explained. He sounded English. "It almost seems as if the dog knows me. I walk them. That is, I am a professional dog walker, and she looks like an old client."

"Her name is Blackball," Bliss said quickly. "I've never used a dog walker. I just got her."

He rubbed Blackball under her chin. "Then it's just my irresistible charm."

In an effort to distract him from Blackball, not to men-tion blackmail, Bliss pointed to the five creatures lying on the floor and filling half the room. "Are those clients?"

He nodded. "The people who own them work. The task of airing them and taking them to their appointments falls to unemployed actors such as myself."

"You're an actor?"

"You look heartbroken."

"My parents are actors."

"Poor child. Who are they?"

"Dan Bowman and Polly Prentice."

"Polly is in my class at the Actors Lab. We're just starting work on a scene together." He held up the script. "*Private Lives.*"

In the last few days Bliss had heard Polly singing "Someday I'll find you" in the shower, and at breakfast looking off into space and asking Bliss if she took "one lump or two," of imaginary sugar from an imaginary silver bowl. "Are you English?"

"No," he smiled, "Affected American."

Taken off guard, Bliss laughed. "Have you worked yet?"

"College theater, summer stock. I was in the Triangle show."

"Princeton."

"One year at any rate. I'm on a leave of absence, so to speak. What about yourself? Are you in the theater?"

Bliss shook her head, "High school. After that I'm going to Vassar. One day I'll be a psychologist and make enough money to buy the best tickets to any show I like. That is as close as I ever plan to get to a theater."

"What conviction. If only we could isolate it and inject it, we'd have a vaccine for the Theater Bug. Afflicted souls like myself could be helped. I would go back to school. My parents would jump for joy." His light intelligent eyes narrowed and softened. He seemed to be appraising her in some way. Bliss felt a hot blush. "It's a pity," he said out loud to himself. "You look like a young Kate Hepburn. Good bones and angles and that tilt of the head. Even your coloring."

Her blush was turning to a fever rash when a receptionist told Bliss to step inside with Blackball.

"She's a healthy dog, between six months and a year," said Delphi Pilpel crisply, running efficient fingers over Blackball's head and torso. In her white coat, she was the image of a cool professional woman. She had administered shots and taken Blackball's weight and temperature. "Bring her in whenever you have a question about her health." She took off her glasses, causing her eyes to cross slightly. Her voice grew a bit husky. "I had such a good time last night. Please tell your father. And of course there won't be any charge."

"I'll tell him."

Delphi reached over the examining table and took Bliss's elbow in her hand. "Is he involved with a particular woman at the moment?"

"He's usually involved with someone." Bliss paused and then decided to say what she wanted to. "Someone young and skinny and dumb. That's his type."

"You're telling me not to get my hopes up."

Bliss nodded.

"Thank you." She smiled. "But I always have to work harder than other people for what I want. I'm used to it. Other people are smarter and wittier and prettier. I had to take my veterinary boards three times. But I got here. Sometimes I am successful."

"Good luck," Bliss said and was surprised to realize she meant it.

6

Walking home along Sixth Avenue, Bliss carefully avoided the route that would take her near the brownstone house Blackball had pulled her to. The sidewalks thronged with rush hour crowds and last-minute shoppers. Idly Bliss began to wonder how many of them had taken the SATs and what scores they had received. A woman in a smart black coat, carrying a leather briefcase, with thin horn-rimmed glasses on her nose surely had scored in the high seven hundreds. A gangly boy waiting for the bus with his jacket flapping struck her as a dull three twenty, unless he had a genious for math and broke all existing records. Passing the newsstand reminded her that housebound Polly would be longing for the *Times* and its crossword puzzle. The daily puzzle was Polly's passion. She would crow her triumphant "Finished!" within half an hour of having attacked it with a ball-point. As Bliss placed her quarter on the plastic counter top, she noticed a girl of about eight standing a few feet away. The girl was staring at her with such a fixed gaze that it made Bliss start. The child had a narrow face, eyes with dents like bruises under them, and a sallow complexion. Wisps of ochre-colored hair escaped from the hood of her green jacket. Her gloveless hands were plunged into pockets that had begun to tear loose. Bliss tucked the paper under her arm. She walked briskly for three blocks, determined not to look over her shoulder. But when she glanced uptown to cross the avenue, the girl was half a block back, still watching.

Polly looked as if she hadn't budged since the day before. The only changes were that the tray was loaded with tea bags and the mounds of legal pad paper had drifted like snow from the table to the floor and sofa.

"I bought you a paper."

Polly blew a kiss. Her nose was red and her eyes teary. "I think you should go back to Dan's. I'm not over this."

"My books and notes are here. I can fix us both some supper. I don't want to keep going back and forth."

Polly sank happily back on her cushions. "You remind me of Grandma, the way you're so competent and take care of people."

"Your infantilism makes grown-ups of us all," said Bliss.

"Goo goo gaa gaa," Polly cooed, accepting the paper with a smile.

"I met somebody from your class at the Lab. He was at the vet's office waiting with a bunch of dogs. He says you're doing a scene together."

"That divine Colin Bragg. He's terribly good. What did you think of him? Isn't he handsome? He's only twenty. Doesn't he have something? Did he say anything about ME?"

34

"He said that *I* reminded him of the young Katharine Hepburn."

"I wonder if that means that *I* remind him of the mature Katharine Hepburn."

In the kitchen Bliss rummaged among the cans on the shelf.

"Psychologist, Horney, five letters," Polly called.

"Karen."

"Good girl."

Bliss hated crossword puzzles. From the time she was little Polly had tried to engage her in word games. "My life would be complete if only I'd had a kid who'd play with me." But Bliss wouldn't. She loathed Scrabble and Spill 'n Spell. She did not like to think of words in those contexts. Words were to be made into thoughts and pictures and evocations, not numerical points with which to score. Now it seemed to her that the SATs loomed over her like a great big word game. Only the number of your score was the number on a price tag affixed to the brain. What have we here? Six hundred? Seven hundred? Eight hundred? Sold, eight hundred, to the Best Schools in the Country. She opened a can of minestrone and one of lentil and dumped them into a pot. She found half a loaf of bread, which she sliced and toasted. There was a droopy head of lettuce and a few radishes. She put them in cold water, then shook them out and sliced them into a bowl.

When she entered the living room with soup, bread, and salad on a tray, Polly was nearly finished with the puzzle. She sat up and arranged the pillows behind her back. Bliss set the tray on her knees. "Someone called you last night. I gave her Dan's number."

"Sibyl Oaks."

"That was it." Polly tasted the soup. "Would she by any chance be related to Lyman Oaks?"

"Who's he?"

"Only the hottest producer on Broadway."

"I don't know."

"Find out."

"Do you seriously think an acquaintance's father could have any effect on your career, Pol?"

"Listen, sweetheart, stranger things have happened."

"Polly, when will you stop stargazing and grow up? When will you stop thinking of life as the plot to some cheap romantic novel or movie from the nineteen forties, with everything meshing to make a happy ending?"

"I would rather see my life as the plot of a movie or novel," said Polly sadly, "than a dreary chapter out of one of those books your Granny gave you to read." She blew her nose. "We made a mistake with you. At an age when I should have been reading you fairy tales I was pushing *The Boys' and Girls' Splitsville Manual,* and *The Kids' Divorce Book,* and *How to Live with Your Divorced Mommy.* Your idea of a fairy godmother is a social worker who tells you it is unrealistic to expect a pumpkin to turn into a golden coach. All that happens to pumpkins is they rot and stink up the joint. There are no Prince Charmings, baby. Royalty is teetering and charm is a superficial defense mechanism."

"*Every Child's Book on Divorce* saved my life."

"Maybe it's time to branch out. Romantic, mysterious, amazing things *do* happen. You have to be on the lookout for them."

"Ahh, True Romances — the latest from Harlequin Books."

"You could start with Grimm and Andersen." Polly

looked over her shoulder. "Actually you could start with closing the curtain. There's a draft on my back."

Bliss went to the window and reached for the broken curtain pull. Across the street, on the corner of the square that faced their building, stood the child in the green jacket, shivering and hunch shouldered. When she saw Bliss in the window, she squinted her eyes. Then she turned and walked toward the farthest side of the square and without stopping crossed the street and rounded the corner.

Bliss drew the curtain. "Polly, I think someone is following me."

"Mmmmm."

"A little girl of about eight. She trailed me home and now she's just leaving the square."

"Weird," Polly sniffled. "Like a novel or a play." They both looked at Blackball, who was vigorously licking her paw. "Let's not let our imaginations run away with us. Maybe it's just that you're paranoid."

Bliss went back to the kitchen to eat her own supper. She wasn't paranoid. She remembered something. In the instant before the shade had been drawn shut in the window of the brownstone house with the red door, she had seen a small face pressed to the pane. The face of the child. She had been followed to Dan's by something green. The green jacket of the child.

On Fridays Partridge Mellon closed at one o'clock. Bliss
went home with Sibyl Oaks.

"I never brought anyone from school before," Sibyl
said. "If my mother throws rose petals in your path, you'll
know why. For six years, it's been hand-wringing and
'Where are your friends?'"

The apartment was vast, a penthouse overlooking the
East River primarily and a great deal of Manhattan inci-
dentally. There were paintings under lights on the walls
and Georgian antique pieces of furniture on the carpets.

"If you're impressed by all this," Sibyl told Bliss as she
led her through two gallerys and a dining room, breakfast
room, and butler's pantry into the kitchen, "you're abso-
lutely right. It took Mr. Lyman Oaks three wives to get to
my mother's sense of pretentious bad taste. They were
made for each other."

"He's not your father?"

"He adopted me. Not that he likes kids; he likes to

acquire things. I was cheap. I would have been penniless little Sibyl Deutch, if not for Mommy's windfall."

In the kitchen, which was powder blue, stainless steel, and immense, one uniformed maid was washing and slicing vegetables at the sink, while another sat at a table drinking coffee. A bearded, bespectacled young man of about twenty leaned against the sink snatching washed carrot sticks out of a colander almost as quickly as they were placed in it.

"Hold off, Mr. Howard," said the housekeeper. "I'm getting nowheres. Where'd you learn to eat, anyway?"

"Zoo," he said through full cheeks.

"Howie, this is Bliss Bowman. I was just telling her how our parents' match was made in heaven."

"The heaven with the great big cash register in it." He extended his hand. "Hello, Blissful Joy. I've admired your name on the class list for many years." Bliss wondered if it was his easy assurance that made him look so familiar.

"What do we have to eat?" Sibyl poked around in the colander.

"Who are you kidding, Sib? You've not been observed in that act since last New Year's. At the time I believe it was a bread stick."

Sibyl took a box out of the refrigerator. "Ah, something from Dumas." She put it on the table. "Cheesecake."

"Don't touch that thing, it's for Mrs. Oaks's tray that I was supposed to have brought to the library ten minutes ago," said the maid who was drinking coffee.

As if to make her point, the intercom on the wall buzzed sharply.

The woman roused herself and began to select cups and saucers to set on a tray. "What'd she say — two, three cups, Mrs. McAddam, you recall?"

"I am the housekeeper here, Jessie. I don't serve trays."

The sharp sound of high heels approaching on the parquet silenced them.

"Where is that tray, Jessie?" Mrs. Oaks said at the door to the kitchen. "We are waiting for our coffee." She saw Bliss and Sibyl and blinked. "Oh Sibyl, when did you get home? I didn't hear you come in."

"I am so thin Mom, I slip through the cracks. This is Bliss Bowman. She saved my life in chemistry. Could I reward her with some cheesecake?"

Mrs. Oaks extended her small, bony, jeweled, enameled fingers for Bliss to shake. She was a thin, tightly wired woman. Her face was painted and her hair arranged in such a way as to give the impression of having been assembled out of a silk-lined box. "There are cookies from Rigo and some tarts from Jean Claude in the bread bin. Mrs. McAddam will show you." She turned to the housekeeper. "It won't do the way this luncheon has been served, Mrs. McAddam. Mr. Oaks is annoyed. It is your responsibility to see that Jessie brings in the tray when I ask."

"I have my own work," came the reply.

"So do we all." Mrs. Oaks looked somewhat intimidated. "I work very hard myself." She noticed Howard for the first time. "Eating again? If you'd gone away to college you'd have saved us a mint."

When she had left the kitchen Jessie, who had kept busy over the preparation of the tray, burst out laughing. "What does she do?"

"Today it was the leg waxer."

"Oh, that's hard."

"Then the hair setter."

"Poor thing."

"And then the shopping."

"How does she bear it?"

"The question is how will you bear it when you're canned?"

"They told me at the agency she goes through girls at a rate of one a week. I figured I wouldn't be here long."

"That's the truth. The only ones they keep are me and Nurse."

"Who's the baby?"

"I am," Sibyl laughed. "Hadn't you noticed?" She loaded a plate with an assortment of tarts, poured out two large glasses of milk, and put them on a tray. "Nurse speaks French. Mommy keeps her around to class up her act." Bliss followed Sibyl out a louvered door. They walked down a long carpeted corridor whose walls were hung with signed photographs of actors, directors, conductors, and producers. Sibyl's room was yellow, blue, and white. It featured a canopied bed and several delicately made pieces of antique furniture.

"As you know, I don't eat," she said, placing the tray on her dresser. "So help yourself." She flopped on the silk brocade bed, and put her feet up. Leaning back into the pillows, she watched Bliss. "I've been observing you for four years, Bowman," she said. "You fascinate me. You and Sewel. You work your tails off. What for?"

"I want to go to Vassar. I want to be a clinical psychologist."

"Why Vassar?"

"My mother went there."

"So? My mother went to Bensonhurst High."

"She took me to visit once." Bliss did not feel like describing the day Polly had taken her to Vassar. She didn't know how to tell about the flowering trees and the stone buildings and the serenity and stability that seemed to emanate from them. The girls she had seen appeared

41

jaunty and clever. Even Polly had become confident and focused for a few hours.

"How do you stand those idiots at school?" She looked over Bliss's shoulder. "Hi, Howie — you know Mother said you can't come in here."

"Even with a chaperone?" Howard leaned in the door, smiling.

"Bliss is telling me how she keeps trucking."

"Leave the girl alone," Howard said. "Stop picking on people." He came into the room and helped himself to one of the tarts. "You're in danger of going through life like Mike Wallace, challenging everybody to justify themselves."

"I'm sorry." Sibyl sat up. "What do normal girls do on after-school dates? Set each other's hair? Try on lipstick?"

"I wouldn't know," Bliss said icily.

"Julie and Nina and Francesca get stoned."

"So I've heard."

"Christine and Susu listen to each other's records, talk about horses, and gossip about Julie and Nina and Francesca."

Bliss began to drink her milk.

"Nora and Abigail eat and gossip about Christine and Susu and Julie and Nina and Francesca. You and Jenny Sewel gossip about all of us and call it psychology."

"I'm getting out of here," said Howard. But he didn't go.

Bliss sat down on a puffy little silk-covered rocker and wished she hadn't come.

"Seriously. How do you get along every frigging day of the week? What do you look forward to? How do you stand it? What can you take seriously?"

"My dog, for one."

"Your which?"

42

"Ever since I found her, I look forward to going home," Bliss said in her most even therapeutic voice. "I have to feed her and walk her and give her time. Even *you* couldn't reduce her to nonsense. If you did she'd die."

"What are you telling me? To get a dog?"

"Yes."

"Oh God." Sibyl rolled onto her side and began to laugh in a very odd way. "I thought a lover, or maybe two, but a dog! Howard, could you learn to bark?"

"I wasn't joking." Bliss stood up. She was hot and angry. She did not like to be put on. "I thought you asked me a serious question. I gave you a serious answer." Actually she had tried to deal with Sibyl as if she were a patient. She never anticipated that a patient would crack up over her advice.

"She knows you weren't joking," Howard said softly. He was watching his stepsister trying to regain her composure.

"I have to go." Bliss looked at her watch.

"Yeah, I know," Sibyl choked with laughter. "You have to walk your dog." She followed Bliss to the door. "Next time we'll set each other's hair and listen to records."

Next time, Bliss thought going down in the elevator, there won't be a next time.

8

There were voices coming from the apartment as Bliss climbed the stairs. She opened the door. Over Blackball's greeting, she heard Polly in the living room: "What have you been doing lately? During these last years?"

A man answered, "Traveling about. I went round the world, you know, after —"

"Yes, yes, I know. How was it?"

"The world?"

"Yes."

"Oh, highly enjoyable."

"China must be very interesting."

"Very big, China."

"And Japan —"

"Very small."

Polly and Colin Bragg were standing in the center of the room holding their scripts. They were gazing out over the sofa at an imaginary moonlit Mediterranean sea, from the terrace of an imaginary hotel in the south of France. They were Elyot and Amanda out of the imagination of Mr. Noel Coward. Neither of them noticed that Bliss had entered the room.

"Come on, come on, don't waste time."

"Oughtn't we to leave them notes or something?"

"No, no no, we'll telegraph from somewhere on the road."

"Darling, I daren't, it's too wicked of us. I simply daren't."

Polly walked quickly toward the window. Colin followed her and without warning (at least to Bliss) seized her in his arms and leaned her so far back that she lost her balance.

"I think we shouldn't dip into that so much," Polly said. "I get dizzy. Oh —" She saw Bliss. "Sweety, you know Colin Bragg."

"Hallo again." He bowed.

"I didn't mean to interrupt."

"We were about to break. We've done the scene six times."

"Backbreaking work," Bliss said to her instant regret.

"Challenging," Colin corrected her.

"If Bliss thinks we're good enough maybe she'll tell Lyman Oaks and he'll run a revival," Polly said.

"Lyman Oaks? Do you know him?"

"If having had a glass of milk in the same apartment where he was eating lunch means I know him, I know him."

"What's the daughter like?" Polly sat down on the sofa and took off her shoes.

"She's a very dear anorexic. You'd really like her."

"Howard Oaks is a decent fellow," said Colin. "He was

a year behind me at the Lakeville school. I think he's at Columbia now."

Bliss was silent and somewhat ashamed of having been flippant.

"I'm going to make tea." Polly got up and left the room quickly.

Bliss realized she was stuck with Colin Bragg.

"Your mother tells me you're at Partridge Mellon. Do you like it?"

"The teaching is very good. I don't have much to do with the girls."

"I shouldn't think so." He lit a cigarette and sat down. "Squeaky-clean hair, to bed at ten, all the memorized points of view of the world's top ten thinkers. How do you bear it?"

"I think of it as a way to get something I really want."

"I could never understand that. I like to enjoy what I'm doing. I believe the present is important. I don't see why one should have to suffer through it, at least not in high school. However, I know I am a shallow hedonist."

Bliss was silent.

"Still" — he blew out smoke — "I can't see it. Why on earth, in a city this large and diverse, should a girl like you choose to restrict herself to the company of that small and narrow bunch. They can only hurt and reject you."

"They don't," said Bliss hotly. "I don't let them."

"Well then, good for you. You're very strong. I just wonder what the point of it is. You could be in a place where you would be socially comfortable AND learning. Surely it need not be a question of one or the other."

"Partridge Mellon is the most prestigious school in the city."

"Ohhhhh," he drew the word out with knowing implication. "And that is important to you, Bliss?"

46

"Not to me." She was flustered. She had not meant to appear shallow. "But it is to the rest of the world."

"And you think that it is very important what the rest of the world thinks? Partridge Mellon, the prestige school. Like Mark Cross, the prestige handbag, or Vuitton the prestige suitcase? Do you get an elegant little monogram *P.M.* to tack on the corner of your brain when you graduate?"

"I wasn't talking about handbags and suitcases. I was talking about an education."

"You were talking about prestige. What the world thinks and the labels that impress it, not about personal judgment and personal achievement."

Polly came in with a tray of cups and tea and cookies.

"I'm making myself very unpopular with your daughter," said Colin. "Though her dog adores me." Blackball had leaped to his feet, wagging her tail and licking his shoes with anxious affection. "I'll say one thing, Bliss, I don't know about Partridge Mellon, but this little dog is prestige from ears to tail."

The telephone's ring sent Polly flying down the hall to the kitchen. In the voice she used for Amanda she called out, "Mr. Howard Oaks, for Blissful Bowman."

When Bliss got on the phone Howard said, "Was the person who answered the phone an actress?"

"I'm sorry."

"Don't apologize."

"I meant for myself."

He laughed softly, and cleared his throat. "Mr. Howard Oaks requesting that Blissful Bowman meet him next Saturday to help select a dog for his sister's birthday."

"Blissful Bowman accepts with pleasure."

"I'm glad Sibyl brought you home. She wasn't laughing at you by the way."

"I know that," said Bliss, who knew no such thing.

"We'll talk about it next week."

When she hung up, Bliss immediately dialed Jenny. "You know that facet of our development that we've been worried about?"

"Mmmm." Jenny was eating something.

"Well I'm about to deal with it."

"You mean a meaningful peer relationship with the opposite sex?"

"Yup, an MPRWOS."

"You mean you've got a boy friend?"

"He's Sibyl's brother. Mature, intelligent, and a freshman at Columbia. We have a date."

"Now maybe something will happen to me," Jenny said thinly.

"If you want it to, and are ready for it, emotionally, it will."

There was a silence in which Jenny breathed ominously. "Boy, you really are something. If you weren't my best friend there are times when I could start to hate you."

"Because of an MPRWOS?"

"Because you act as if you had this dumb little checklist. Good School, Good Grades, Good Boy Friend, Good College. I suppose Howard Oaks advances you three boxes past GO. I just wonder where you think you're going. If you aren't a self-satisfied, smug snob, you certainly do a good job of imitating one."

"You know it's all a cover for my insecurities," Bliss wailed.

"Okay," Jenny said, mollified. "Ask Howard Oaks if he's got a friend."

Polly poked her head around the door. "Could you do us a huge favor and cue us? We're almost word perfect."

"Got to go," Bliss told Jenny. "If he doesn't have a friend I don't want to know him."

Polly and Colin took their places in the center of the living room. Polly struck a languid slouching pose and stared at the wall behind the sofa, over Bliss's head.

"Whose yacht is that?"

"The Duke of Westminster's I expect. It always is."

"I wish I were on it."

"I wish you were too."

"There's no need to be nasty."

Bliss followed them in the script. She tried to keep her eyes on the page, but it was difficult not to watch. Colin was smooth, understated and elegant. She couldn't take her eyes off him.

"You're looking very lovely, you know, in this damned moonlight. Your skin is clear and cool . . ."

Clear and cool? Bliss looked at Polly's skin. It was creased and dull. She should not be playing scenes opposite Colin Bragg, not even for an acting class.

Colin's voice, so seductive and easy, went on: "More than any desire anywhere, deep down in my deepest heart I want you back again — please —"

In a moment they were in each other arms.

"Excuse me." Bliss stood up abruptly. "That was very good, perfect."

They drew apart.

"I have to walk Blackball." She bolted from the room, leashed the dog, and grabbed her jacket. Polly in love was bad enough. Polly in love with a man half her age was a disaster Bliss could not bear to think of, much less sit and watch. Freud was right. Actors were children. Furthermore, Polly was destined to play out her infantile role again and again. With every passing year it would grow

49

more pathetic. An infatuation with Colin Bragg was precisely what Bliss would have predicted for her mother. She didn't like Colin. He was vain. He enjoyed putting people on the defensive. He passed judgment on her life and her school and even her dog. Everything about him alarmed her.

"Hey, wait up." Colin sprinted down the stairs after her. "I have to walk about half-a-dozen dogs myself."

Bliss waited on the landing, resenting it.

"I never saw anybody run out of a reading so fast. We must have been terrible."

"You were." They both stopped on the stairwell.

"Why?" Colin suddenly looked very young and vulnerable.

"You weren't together. Polly was out of a play by Ibsen or Chekhov. She was all wrong."

"If that's true, it's my fault. I have to find ways to make her look better. A scene like that is a duet. What were the most obvious differences? Movement? Diction? Voice?"

Bliss shrugged. "You were animals of two different species." She stopped herself from saying that he was a gazelle and Polly a water buffalo. They walked slowly down the rest of the stairwell.

"Thanks," he said.

"What for?"

"You have a good ear. More than that." He looked away from her, his face unsure and his gesture gauche. "You're honest."

Standing on the top step of the outside stoop, Bliss fastened her collar button. Beneath a ginko on the near corner of the square stood the child in the green jacket. When she saw them she smiled and waved. In a confused instant Bliss realized the recipient of the greeting was Colin Bragg. He tipped his charming head in the girl's direction, whereupon she turned on her heel and ran off at full speed. "Do you know her?" asked Bliss.

"In a manner of speaking. She's an odd little thing with a tragic sort of life."

"Who is she following, you or me?"

"I can think of a few reasons for her to follow either of us, can't you?"

"No." Bliss thrust out her jaw. "I can't."

His expression was quizzical and puzzled. He seemed about to say something, but changed his mind. "Then you're less honest with yourself than you've been with me." He doffed an imaginary hat. "Thank you again, Bliss. I come off the winner." He waved and hurried away.

9

Saturday morning when Bliss arrived with Blackball at Dan's for the weekend, she found him in a frenzy of food preparation.

"My new friend is coming for dinner," Dan said, not looking up from whatever it was he was beating with a whisk. "Did Polly tell you?"

"No, did *you* tell Polly?"

"Oh Blisstix, you know I tell Polly all sorts of things, on the phone. She's my Dial Pal."

"Who's the lucky lady?" Bliss bent to Blackball, hoping not to reveal the odd wrench that still overcame her when she was confronted with her parents' fondness for each other. Why couldn't they have tried a little harder and made a real effort to stay together?

"Trianna Gregory," Dan said, "is the lucky lady."

"The one in the blouse ad?"

Dan nodded proudly. "Polly told me you've got a date

this afternoon. Why don't you bring him back for dinner?"

"I don't think so." Bliss had spent hours thinking about this date with Howard. She saw it as if it were a short story titled "First Date," with an illustration of a young couple in hazy pastels, appearing in a magazine called *Normal Life*. Returning home with this First Date in Normal Life did not include watching one's father court a blouse ad.

"Then we'll be stuck with tons of leftovers. Veal Orloff, most complicated thing I ever cooked."

"What happened to Delphi Pilpel?"

"Lovely lady. Never sent a bill."

"She really likes you, Dan."

"What else is new?" He took the whisk out of the bowl and plopped it in the sink.

"For two weeks I've been followed by a kid in a green jacket. She tails me at a distance of half a block and waits outside our building and stares at our windows."

"Why?"

"Blackball pulled me to her front door."

"To Green Jacket's front door?" He began to stir heavy cream into the top of a double boiler.

"Yes. Green Jacket saw me from her window. She followed me over here. The next day she followed me from here back to Polly's. She must have waited for me to come home from school. Now she's my shadow."

"Maybe you're her class project at a progressive school. If she wants Blackball, the precinct or the ASPCA would have called you back."

"I never reported her missing, Dan."

Dan looked up from his pot, one of his rare direct gazes over the rim of his half glasses. "You didn't?"

"I didn't."

"How un-Blissful."

"If that kid wants Blackball back, she'll have to kidnap her."

"Dognap. What does Polly say about all this?"

"Polly is busy. She's involved with a boy. They're working on a scene. You know Polly." Bliss watched him closely, hoping for a reaction. She wanted to get him jealous. Claim Polly while you can. Win her back, she may be lost to you forever. Stop playing with Blouse Ads and wrest your lawful spouse from Colin Bragg.

Dan's face fell into lines of sadness. "Yes, I know Polly. Poor Blissy. What troublesome parents the stork brought you."

The picture of an old wizened little Bliss being brought two baby parents made them both smile.

"But look how well you've done, sweet pea," Dan cheered himself up. "You're so mature and confident. A real grown-up. Who's this afternoon's lucky fellow?"

"His name is Howard Oaks."

"Is he by any chance related to Lyman Oaks, the hottest producer on Broadway?"

"What if he were?"

"You could put in a good word for your old man."

"Oh Dan," Bliss shook her head. "Things like that don't happen."

"Anything can happen," Dan insisted, "if you think young." He picked up his spoon and waved it in the air for emphasis. Poised by the stove, his bright blue eyes eager and smiling, his body graceful and erect, he reminded Bliss of someone. Who? Polly, that was who.

She met Howard Oaks for lunch at a restaurant called the Soupery, which was across the street from a pet shop they planned to look into

54

As soon as they were seated at a table near the glass-windowed corner, Bliss wished fervently that someone, anyone from Partridge Mellon would walk past and see them. Or better still, would come into the restaurant. "Hi," she would wave, "I'd like you to meet Howard Oaks, my friend at Columbia."

"I don't know how well you know Sibyl," Howard was saying.

"She sees to it that nobody knows her."

"You're right. However, she likes you. She talks about you a lot. My friend Bliss this, my friend Bliss that."

"That's dumb."

"She's not dumb. She got a near-perfect score on her PSATs."

"She says she got it by reducing everything to nonsense. She told me there are only one or two things in life worth taking seriously."

"Her problem is she hasn't found them yet. That's the reason she admires you. You have plans and hopes. You take everything seriously."

A brisk young waitress set a bowl of sliced bread and a crock of butter between them and took their orders for eggplant soup.

Howard folded his hands self-consciously on the table and gazed unhappily at them. "She's very smart."

"Who?"

"Sibyl. Her mother, my father's present wife, is a vapid, silly woman. No one has understood Sibyl. No one has wanted to deal with her."

Neither did Bliss. Interested though she might be in adolescent pathology, she wished Howard could focus his attention on herself instead. "I met someone who knows you."

He didn't seem curious or even surprised by Colin

Bragg's name. "I liked Col. He was one of the school's successes. Everyone assumed he was going places in the theater. What's taking him so long?"

"So long?"

"I was kidding." When he smiled, his long face above the beard broke into lines that struck Bliss as familiar. Had she seen him in a dream? or a previous life? "You said your mother was an actress." The bowls of soup were set before them.

"My father is in the theater too."

"We have something in common. I've grown up around theater people. Although what my father does has more to do with investment than art, my mother —" He looked as if a cloud had passed over his eyes. "My mother is, or was, or may be an actress, like yours."

"Is, was, or may be?"

He held his spoon to the side of his bowl and looked into it as if taking his words off it. "It's hard to know. My mother's disappeared."

"Disappeared?" Bliss realized that she was foolishly repeating what he said.

"Disappeared is a word that describes someone or thing that is gone from its proper place. If my mother's proper place was the house she shared with her present husband and their child, then I must say she has disappeared without leaving a trace."

"Have you looked?"

"She is an officially listed Missing Person. However, a forty-some-year-old known eccentric who has gone out to walk her dog on a winter afternoon and not returned is hardly the sort of case to work our New York Police Department to a froth of energy."

"Do they suspect foul play?"

"Do you mind if we change the subject?" Howard

smiled wanly. "As a budding psychologist, I'm sure the story holds immense fascination for you, but as the runaway's son, it slightly drags me down."

The subject that certainly did not "drag him down" was that of his stepsister. Finally Bliss gave up trying to change it. In the middle of a detailed description of Sibyl's eating habits, Howard interrupted himself, "Speak of the devil," he exclaimed. Through the clear windowpane, crossing the street in the bright sunlight, heading for their very corner was Sibyl Oaks. Howard tapped on the glass and waved his arms wildly. When she saw them Sibyl rolled her eyes and jumped up and down in a pantomime of surprise and delight. In a flash she had come through the door of the restaurant, pulled a chair out from a nearby table, squeezed herself between them, and pushed both elbows among the glasses and bowls. "*Quelle* coincidence," she beamed at Howard.

"What are you doing here?" he said as if he hadn't seen her for months.

"You know I have the orthodontist across the street every Saturday." By way of demonstration she pulled her lips apart with her fingers to show a thin wire encasing her teeth.

Howard snapped his fingers. "Of course, of course."

"What are you two doing after lunch?" Sibyl crumbled a piece of bread between her knobby fingers and drizzled crumbs onto the butter.

"We're going to buy a dog for Blissful's dog," Howard said quickly. "Would you like to join us?"

"Oh dear." Sibyl made a great fuss squinting at her oversize wristwatch and winding it. "I don't know. What would Bliss think of me, horning in on my brother's date."

"Let's ask her."

"Would you think I was weird if I tagged along?"

"Would you think she was weird?" Howard repeated so earnestly that Bliss nearly loved him for the way he tolerated this sick interfering stepsister. He smiled at Bliss, even winked. "Help me out," he seemed to be saying.

Bliss nodded recalling her wish that someone anyone from P.M. see them together. She decided to be more circumspect in her wishes.

On the street Howard walked between them, holding both firmly by the arm so they had to slide diagonally through the crowds on Lexington Avenue. They were giddy and laughing, as if part of some daffy parade.

"If we learn to kick we could join the Rockettes," Sibyl hooted.

"Not me," Howard said. "It's a sexist group."

"You'd be a test case. If we won would you shave your legs?"

"Just one. It would be my token leg."

Bliss listened to them in envy. They were so familiar, more so than she was with Jenny. They seemed to speak as well as move in unison. Their minds were linked and as in tune as their steps. An old regret seized her. Why did she have to be an only child?

They entered a pet shop, the front of which was mobbed with Saturday browsers. "What sort of dog does your dog want?" Sibyl asked.

"I'm not sure." Bliss looked at Howard for help.

"Didn't you say small and white?"

Bliss nodded.

"Oh, loooook." Sibyl pointed at a cage in the back of the shop. "That is the most adorable thing I've ever seen in my life." She began to push her way toward it. "If I were your dog, that is the only pet I would consider."

They lined up in front of the puppy's cage and watched

it run toward them on wobbly young legs. Its dark eyes caught the light. Its lemon nose poked through the mesh. Sibyl held up her hand for nibbling. "What is it?"

"Maltese," a salesman said. "And she's sold."

"Oh." Sibyl was tragic. "Dreadful."

Bliss noticed that Howard mirrored her changing moods. He was right behind her on a roller coaster, from joy to misery and back.

"But what's tha-at?" Once again Sibyl was pushing through the crowds. She had seen another cage. "You are the sweetest creature I ever saw in my life," she told the puppy. "I'd give my flea collar for you."

"Is she putting us on?" Bliss whispered to Howard as Sibyl clapped her hands and pulled back to yet another cage.

"I change my mind. I like cats better." Kneeling to the floor, Sibyl began to croon baby-talk at a sleeping angora kitten.

Bliss withdrew. She leaned against a case of collars and leashes and watched Howard watching Sibyl. They were circling the shop together. At each cage Sibyl changed her mind and declared her love for another animal. After ten minutes even Howard looked tired and confused. Sibyl's high, affected voice was beginning to show signs of strain. They left the shop, to the obvious relief of the salesmen and customers.

"It's only three o'clock," Sibyl said brightly. "What are we going to do now?"

When Bliss turned to Howard in desperation, she was amazed to see how compassionately he regarded Sibyl. Bliss was more impressed than ever by Howard Oaks.

"I thought we'd try another pet shop down in the village," he said gaily. "I've heard great things about the place."

On the bus downtown, Sibyl looked suddenly stricken. "Oh God, what am I doing here anyway?" she said.

"We're going to a pet shop," Howard reminded her gently.

"But I'm horning in on your first date with Bliss," she wailed. "I'm awful. Please tell me to get lost. I mean it."

No she doesn't, Bliss thought, and knew that the rest of the afternoon was Sibyl's.

It seemed to take forever to find the pet shop, and when they did Sibyl fell in love with a snake. "I'd take it everywhere with me. I'd never let it out of my sight. I adore it."

"Your mother would never allow you to have it."

"She's never allowed me to have anything I love."

Bliss watched them exchange a long look. Howard's gaze, kind and sympathetic; Sibyl's, burning and angry. Bliss had never met a young man like Howard. He was psychologically aware and mature without being overbearing or pompous.

"Anyway, this is boring." Sibyl shrugged. "What I really want to do is go home with Bliss and see her dog."

"You can't!" Bliss panicked.

"Why not?"

"I'm at my father's for the weekend."

"Don't push it, Sib," Howard said.

"Isn't your father's place home?"

"Not the same."

"We'll just walk you to your door and leave you there," Howard reassured her.

Their mood on the short walk to Dan's was sober, in fact depressed.

"Can I see the lobby?" Sibyl sulked. "I mean, will you

be mortified if I step into the lobby of your father's building?"

"You can see the lobby."

In the lobby, Sibyl eyed the dark little elevator. "If I step into the elevator, will you go into shock?"

"Sibyl, stop it," Howard snapped. It was the first time he showed his exasperation with her.

This pleased Bliss so that she surprised herself by relaxing. "You can come upstairs."

At Dan's floor they were greeted by a wonderful herby cooking smell. "That is the most divine smell on earth," Sibyl cried. "Nobody is going to believe this, but I am starved."

In the kitchen they found Dan mincing garlic and Trianna Gregory propped against the refrigerator like a yardstick in purple velour. She was sipping wine.

"Daddy, this is Sibyl and Howard Oaks."

Dan introduced them all to Trianna, who raised her four long red-tipped fingers in greeting. "Hi ho." She was a classic Dan selection, receiving the classic Dan treatment. Since he wasn't rich, Dan had to give a girl a sense of indulgence in affordable cuts of meat rather than fun furs. From the look of her, Bliss guessed Trianna Gregory lived on celery sticks and amphetamines.

"You've got wonderful bones, and I adore those freckles," she told Bliss. "Do all of you know your signs?"

When she had heard them, her outlined eyes widened. "You realize what this means? I told Dan that I had vibes about tonight. I told him something big was going to happen. I was right."

"You told me there would be one mystery guest and we've got two."

"I told you four romantic destinies would be evolving."

"Four?" Sibyl plopped on the kitchen stool. "This is fantastically neurotic. Do you read the future too, Mr. Bowman?"

"No, but I'm very good at recalling the past. My very first job in the theater was in a Lyman Oaks production. *Volpone.*" Dan turned from the garlic and smiled winningly. "I certainly wish he'd think of me when he's casting his next play."

Bliss certainly wished the linoleum floor of the kitchen would open and swallow her father up, garlic and all. Things couldn't get worse.

"Invite me to dinner, Mr. Bowman," Sibyl said slyly, "and I'll put in a good word for you with the casting office."

Things *could* get worse.

"I thought you came up here to see my dog." Blackball hadn't even come out to greet them.

"That was just an excuse," Sibyl laughed. "I have no interest in animals."

"Set two more places in the dining-room-part-of-the-living-room," Dan said.

Bliss took her time setting the table. She saw Blackball's nose sticking out from under the sofa, and longed to crawl under and keep her company. As she knelt to pat the dark head that protruded another few inches, Howard surprised her by squatting at her side.

"I'm sorry about all this. You didn't want us to come up and now we're staying for dinner. I had no idea Sib would go this far." He stroked Blackball's ear. "If there's a mystery guest, I'll marry your dog." He rested his hand on the hand Bliss held to the dog's snout, and she grew warm with relief. The door bell rang.

From the foyer they heard Delphi Pilpel's clear high voice. "I know I should have called first, but you can always tell me to go away. I found this bottle of Montrechat and thought of the person I'd like to share it with. You. Oh dear. Is this a party?"

"I've cooked enough for five more. Blissful will set another place."

"Don't tell me your sign," Trianna said to Delphi; "let me guess. You're a Capricorn."

"Capricorn?" She looked confused for a moment, then her face brightened. "I see what you mean. Horoscope, mumbo-jumbo, stars and such. No no." She tapped her temple. "My sign is here. Work, effort" — she looked at Dan — "and love."

"Normal life," Bliss thought dismally as she set another place, "is not evolving in my destiny."

10

By one o'clock Sunday afternoon, Dan was still sleeping. Bliss left him a note. "Dear Pops, I did the dishes. Thanks for the dinner." She crossed out "dinner" and wrote "destiny." Then she crossed out "destiny" and wrote "Veal Orloff."

She leashed Blackball and went to Jenny's.

"Are you in love?" Jenny demanded as soon as she opened the door.

"Is it multiple choice, antonyms, analogies, or complete a sentence?"

"Complete a sentence. Bliss Bowman on her first date with Howard Oaks not only fell madly in love but: A. remembered to ask him if he had a friend for chum; B. gorged on oysters and champagne; C. had an attack of nerves and was sent home."

Bliss shook her head. "D. his sister Sibyl tagged along and made All Of The Above Impossible." She hoped

Jenny wouldn't guess that she had completely forgotten to ask about the "friend."

"He *let* Sib do that?" Jenny gave her a quizzical look.

"He is so kind and compassionate and mature." Bliss overlooked Jenny's look. "He handles her beautifully. He even knew how to manage the crazy scene at Dan's." At the thought of that scene, her spirits began to plummet.

"Still . . ." Jenny led Bliss into her room where they lowered themselves onto facing red bean bags. "I wonder why he was so nice about Sib's tagging along. You know they aren't related."

"What are you saying?"

"I don't know." Jenny twirled a lock of long black hair and looked vaguely over Bliss's shoulder and out the window.

"He asked me out. He didn't have to." Bliss leaned forward in the bean bag and started to get up. She took Blackball's leash off the floor where she had let it drop. "I think it would be a good idea if you expressed your jealousy directly and stopped making those indirect annoying allusions. Why don't you say what you think in plain English."

"I don't know what I think." Jenny glared at her.

"It might be a good idea if you made a serious effort to find a meaningful peer relationship with the opposite sex for yourself. You would be less vindictive."

When Bliss let herself out the door, neither she nor Jenny said good-bye.

There was a note stuck under the rim of Polly's peephole with no stamp on the envelope. The writing was that of a child. A round, high script. "Bliss Bo-Man." The note inside was written on loose-leaf paper. "Tell Mommy That I Love Her."

Bliss folded the note into her jacket pocket. Then she

65

took it out, read it again, and as a pain began to spread from the front of her head to the back she refolded it into her skirt pocket.

Polly was in the kitchen. "Colin is coming by to rehearse. He'll have dinner with us first." Bliss noticed that the apartment had been tidied and there were three places set at the table in the foyer.

"He doesn't eat much. His parents don't approve of what he's doing. They didn't want him to drop out of college. They won't help him. He lives in a fleabag some place midtown and supports himself with any odd jobs he can get. Dog walking, bartending, plant sitting. Every penny goes for rent and his classes at the Lab." Polly opened a can of tomatoes as if it would attack her and stood back to drop its contents into the pot of onions and garlic she had begun to brown. "He really likes you, Bliss. He's always asking me about you and commenting on how great you look and what strength and integrity you have."

"Just one big happy family," Bliss mumbled. Had she missed the chapter on "How to Get Along with Your Divorced Mother's Adolescent Boy Friend"?

Colin brought a bottle of wine as well as a recording of Noel Coward and Gertrude Lawrence reading and singing snatches from *Private Lives*.

"Bliss will put it on the machine," Polly said. "I have to deal with my sauce."

Bliss took the record into the living room and set it on the turntable. Colin watched her. The reedy voices of Noel and Gertie reached out from a distance of decades, filling the room with tunes and dialogue.

"Marvelous, magical," Polly rhapsodized from down the hall.

"You don't like it," Colin said to Bliss.

"No."

"Why?"

"It's phony and unnatural. Who are they? Two people with no connection to real life. That's not the way people talk. It's pretending. It's make-believe."

"What's wrong with that? It doesn't hurt anyone. Don't you ever do it?"

"I can't afford to. I have to confront my reality. Nobody else around here does."

"Why are you so hard on Polly?"

"I'm not hard on her. I feel sorry for her. She's like that record. Both my parents live in dreams. Every day they spin new ones. That's what it is to be an actor."

"You sit in judgment on all of us."

"It isn't judgment, it's the way I see it."

He peered at her quizzically. "Can you tell me where you got your dog?"

"I found her on the subway."

"Have you tried to locate her owners?"

Bliss didn't answer.

"I assume you did. You wouldn't purposely avoid confronting reality."

"What do you care?" Bliss said. "Why are you so hard on me?"

He took an awkward step toward her and awkwardly reached for her hand. "Because I care about you." His voice was an unsteady offshoot of itself.

Polly called from the kitchen that dinner was ready.

When they were seated and Colin had poured out the wine, he raised his glass for a toast. "To the Bowman women, intelligent and gifted."

"Gifted at what?" Polly beamed.

"The art of make-believe." When he looked at her, Bliss saw in his eyes the knowing glint of the blackmailer.

"I'm on to you," it seemed to say. "I have known about you ever since I recognized your dog in Dr. Pilpel's waiting room. Don't think you can judge me for this little affair with your mother. Neither of us is perfect."

"As of tomorrow morning, I will not be dealing much in make-believe," Polly sighed. "Office Temps has come up with a new form of prison. Another opening, another show. Another office, another desk. An ad agency, Windham and Lewis." She twirled her spaghetti. "Maybe it's time to chuck the stage. I haven't had a job in the theater for eighteen months."

"You don't mean it, Polly. Why do you say it?" Bliss said.

"Maybe I do mean it. You're the one who is so big on confronting facts. Your message has gotten through. The fact is, I have no career."

"When it comes down to it," Colin interjected, "Bliss believes in very carefully selecting the facts to confront. She picks only the ones she likes."

Bliss could eat no more. The odd note in her pocket and Colin's words combined to accuse her. More than that she was trying to understand her reaction to his taking her hand while they had been in the living room. She couldn't believe the wave of feeling that had suddenly engulfed her. The unconscious, which she had tried to understand in others and control in herself, had suddenly overwhelmed her. She had wished for a moment that she was Polly, and that Colin would take her in his arms as he had her mother in their scene from *Private Lives*. Such a tumult of emotion had been unleashed in that moment as she had not experienced in an entire day with Howard Oaks. She hadn't asked for these feelings. She didn't want them. Not for Colin. Colin was dangerous. He made her feel like a liar and a hypocrite. She could do something about that.

As soon as she had cleared the dishes she leashed Blackball. "Okay, whoever you are," she said gruffly. "It's time to take you home."

At first the dog held back, dug in her feet, and looked truculent. This was not the "usual" time for a walk. But when she sensed where they were going, she began to run. With her ears back and her tail up, an east wind at her back, she pulled Bliss behind her. The small curved street was quiet except for the motor of an occasional car and the rattling of the bare trees against their braces. A silvery television light emanated from the parlor-floor window of the brownstone with the red door. In its areaway a bicycle was chained to the iron gate. Bliss drew in her breath and started to climb the steps. But the door opened. Two figures, their backs half turned to her, appeared in it. They were talking. One was the child with the ochre-colored hair. The other was Howard Oaks.

Before he could see her, Bliss yanked Blackball back, and without stopping for breath pulled the startled dog home.

Her confrontation with reality would have to wait for another time.

11

Bliss read and reread the puzzling anonymous note. What did it mean? Why was Howard visiting the child with the ochre-colored hair? She thought she knew, but it all seemed too fantastic. By the time she got home from school the following day, she could bear her ignorance no longer. She called Colin Bragg. "I have to see you, Colin," she pleaded.

"I'll be under the arch in Washington Square Park with my clients at four," he said.

Low clouds scudded across a sky of dramatic light and dark contrasts. Everything, sky, earth, and buildings, seemed to be in motion, as if turning, casting off, and pushing upward. The trodden patches of grass in the park appeared darker. The tops of buildings were in clear definition against the sky. Bliss felt edgy and vulnerable. The thoughts in her mind were as fitful and elusive as the March wind that tunneled down the Village streets and blustered in the open space of the park.

Colin and five dogs approached her from the opposite side of the arch.

"That girl in the green jacket," Bliss began quickly, "the one who follows me, she sent me a note. She wanted me to tell her mother that she loved her. Last night, because of some of the things you said, I went to return my dog. When I got to the house, Howard Oaks was leaving. I ran away before he could see me."

"What do you want to know, Bliss?"

"Is Blackball that girl's dog?"

"Let's find out," Colin said. "Put her leash down."

All six dogs were sniffing the earth and each other. None of them noticed that their leashes had been dropped. Colin signaled Bliss to follow him several feet away. He climbed a low pile of rocks, raised his hands to his mouth and called, "Sheba."

Only Blackball turned like a shot, and in a series of bounding leaps, stood at his feet, her pink-tongued mouth opened in what looked very much like a smile.

"Sheba," Bliss repeated wretchedly.

"She was a client," said Colin. "The family name is Knight. That little girl who tails you is Louisa. Her mother, the woman who owned the dog, is an actress named Nadine Olson."

"And she is Howard's mother."

Colin nodded. "In January she went to walk her dog and did not return."

"I suppose it's time for me to return her dog," said Bliss. The back of her throat began to close off so quickly that when Colin said he would go with her she could only nod her gratitude.

Louisa Knight opened the door. She was eating a doughnut. She wore a T-shirt and jeans. She looked thinner and paler even than she did in her jacket. A television set blared from somewhere. The light in the narrow entry hall was dim. When Louisa saw Colin and Bliss her face broke into the smile of delight that had haunted Bliss at her first meeting with Howard. "Oh Col," she cried. "You found her."

"Here she is," Bliss croaked. "Sheba."

The girl looked down at Blackball and her face crumpled. "Oh no," she said with disgust.

A woman came through the door at the end of the corridor. She was wiping her hands on a towel. "I thought I heard the bell. Louisa, what is it?" The girl had turned her back to them and leaned into the wall. Her head was buried in her thin arms.

"I think she thought we'd found her mother," said Colin.

"But that was silly. Why on earth would she have an idea like that?"

"Because we've got Sheba." Colin put his hand on Louisa's shoulder. "Did you think Sheba was with your mother?"

She nodded into her arms.

"I found her on the subway," said Bliss kneeling to comfort Blackball, who had begun to tremble and whine, turning her head this way and that, searching for a past mistress and friend. "She was alone. I wanted her for myself. That's why I didn't report her or return her to you. I couldn't stand your following me around."

Louisa half turned. "When I saw you on the street outside our house that day, I knew it was a sign from Mommy. I knew you had a message. I ran after you. I followed you to the apartment house, and the next day I waited for you when I came home from school. Then I followed you to the other house. I saw you in the window.

I checked your name on the mailbox. It said Bowman, Polly and Bliss. I thought if I kept following you, you would take me to Mommy. Mommy gave you Sheba." She looked angrily at the dog. "Sheba makes me wheeze."

"What a spy you've been, Louisa," the woman said in amazement. "All those afternoons when you told me you were going to the library."

When Louisa didn't respond, the woman sighed. "I'm Mrs. Olson, Nadine's mother. We didn't try to locate the dog. Louisa is allergic to her and it was enough for me to come and run this house without adding a dog to it. I'd ask you in, but I see you've got six animals. I'm glad you've taken Sheba. I'm gratified to know that something has been found and is safe." Her eyes began to redden. She tapped the girl on the shoulder. "Say good-bye and thank you, Louisa. These people have been very kind, even if you don't want the dog back."

Louisa spun around so that her angry splotched face was full upon them. "You do know where she is. She gave you Sheba. You saw her and she told you things."

"That isn't true," Bliss shook her head.

"Take me to where you got Sheba," she demanded. "Show me."

"It was a subway car," Bliss said hopelessly.

"Take me to the subway car."

"That's impossible. I don't know which."

"Maybe," Colin began gently, "you could pick Louisa up in the afternoon and show her the station. Then she wouldn't suspect you of lying. She would know something."

Bliss understood. "Okay," she said. "I'll pick you up at three."

Louisa smiled and nodded.

* * *

On the corner of the street, under a sodium lamp that had just come on, they stopped.

"Thank you, Colin, for helping me out."

"Don't thank me. As in the fairy tales, you've been rewarded for seeking out and confronting the truth. Blackball is yours."

Bliss picked the dog up in her arms, receiving Blackball's wet kisses on her cheek. "I'd rather have her than fifty 'lived happily ever afters.' "

"Including a prince?"

"Including a prince."

"Oh well," Colin shrugged and raised his brows in a show of disappointment. "Next time I'll wear my Irish Setter disguise."

On the front steps of her school the following day Bliss saw Jenny surrounded by three girls. Since she had left Jenny's house the previous Sunday they had exchanged nothing more than a clipped greeting. No telephone calls, no lunches. But when Jenny saw her, she waved over Susu Bennet's head and called out. As Bliss approached the group, Susu and Francesca left.

"I have been asked by three people if you are really Howard Oaks's girl," Jenny said.

"How would anybody know?"

"Sib has been the town crier. She is getting invitations to lunch for the description of your father's dinner party. Her favorite subjects are the clairvoyant bra model and the way Howard looked into your eyes. Say, you're turning color."

"She's a blouse model. This is horrible."

"Didn't you want a MPRWOS?"

75

"I didn't want it owned and operated by Sibyl Oaks. She's crazy."

"Crazy? What a way for a budding psychologist to talk. Anorexic, a touch schizophrenic, a little manicky."

"That's what I meant."

"Ho ho," Jenny scoffed.

"You're holding all this against me and it isn't my fault."

Jenny was silent. Her pink lower lip protruded. "I feel as if we were both standing, waiting in the wings, and all of a sudden *you* got called. Why you? Don't they want exotic beauties anymore? What happened to almond-eyed señoritas? Creole lovelies? Half-caste enchantresses? This season it's all bony blondes with dogs."

"What can I do about that?"

Jenny shook her head. "I'm sorry about Sunday. I suppose I am jealous. I know it's not your fault that all these things are happening to you. I just wish you'd stop being so categorical. Howard took you out, equals he's your boy friend. Colin rehearses a love scene with Polly, equals he's her lover. Maybe it's not so simple."

"I know," Bliss wailed. "I don't understand it anymore. It's beyond me. I just wish I had a normal life. I wish Dan would find someone mature and stable and his own age instead of models who read horoscopes. I wish Polly would find a steady job that used her mind instead of dreaming of acting work she'll never get."

"Someone said, watch out what you wish for." Jenny grinned.

At lunch Susu Bennet, Julie Sarton, and Nina Eskind converged on their table. "Sibyl says her brother's madly in love with you," said Susu, blinking her heavy-lidded blue eyes. Her face was blank with awe. Jenny and Bliss always joked about Susu. They called her the "easy weeper." She loved her horse and was only happy when riding it, drawing it, or talking about it. Now it seemed she had a second interest. Romance.

"I don't know what Sib's talking about and neither does she." Bliss opened her lunch bag, trying to conceal the pleasure she was taking from all the attention.

Sibyl herself plunked down on the tabletop. "I know what I'm talking about," she said merrily. "I even know something you don't."

Bliss waited for a moment, chewing, until Sibyl could bear it no longer. "You are meeting Louisa Knight, Howie's other sister, after school today to help her track down her mother."

"I know that," Bliss snapped.

"You don't know that Howie is going to join you."

"How do you know?" Bliss was interested in spite of herself. The girls at the table had turned into a rapt audience, following the conversation as if it were on a stage.

"Louisa called Howie last night and told him all about your going over to her house with your dog that used to be Nadine's. She said you were going to pick her up today after school." Sibyl crossed her legs gingerly at the knee and leaned back on the table. "I'd keep away from that scene if I were you. It's hopeless. Nadine's bats. The kid's not far behind."

Bliss was amazed. Sibyl Oaks calling someone bats.

"When Nadine is up, she's on the other side of the moon. When she's down, she's sitting in the corner counting her tin cans. She gets to thinking she's bad for people and runs out on them. She ran out on Howie. She ran out on his dad. She lives in cheap hotels and rides the subway like that dog. My advice to you is, don't get involved."

"The last time someone gave me that advice, I didn't

listen either," Bliss said, balling up the waxed paper from her sandwich. "I wish you would, Sib."

"Would what?"

"Follow your own advice. Don't get so involved in my business."

Sibyl hopped down from the table, a curious half smile on her lips, and threw back her head. "Your business and my business are the same, Bowman."

Louisa was hopping impatiently from foot to foot, waiting for Bliss on the corner of her street. "My brother Howard says he'll meet us at Cookies and buy us a hot chocolate when we get back."

"What a surprise," said Bliss. She wanted Louisa to trust her. She wanted Louisa to like her. As B. J. Bowman, Ph.D., behind her desk in a sunlit office she would be expert in establishing rapport with young patients. She knew she could help Louisa relinquish her fantasy life and accept reality. "You know that your mother's leaving had nothing to do with you." She took Louisa's hand and walked with her toward the subway.

"Yes it did," Louisa insisted. "We had a fight. She wanted me to wear my green jacket. I said it was too hot. She yelled and screamed and I went to school in my slicker. When I came home she was gone."

"But that was just a coincidence. Your mother's problems had to do with things which you have no part of."

"You mean she couldn't find work and left my dad and wouldn't take her pills?" Louisa looked bored. "I'm going to wear my green jacket till she comes home."

"We don't run people's lives with our superstitions."

"You sound like my therapist."

They went down into the station. As the train came in,

Bliss called over its roar: "We'll go up to Thirty-fourth Street. That's where I saw Sheba. Then we'll get on the downtown train and come home." She was certain that Louisa would be as dejected and disappointed on the trip back as she was cheerful on the trip uptown. However, when they stepped out on the Thirty-fourth Street platform, she seemed delighted by everything she saw and was pleased and satisfied to cross the station to the southbound train. As they went out through the turnstyle at Christopher Street, she grabbed Bliss's hand. "Now I know she'll come back," she said.

Bliss put her arm around Louisa's shoulder. "Real life is not like fairy tales. In real life you have to deal with what you are given and make the best of it." She realized that Louisa wasn't listening. So much for establishing rapport.

Howard sat waiting for them in a corner booth at Cookies, a coffeeshop near Sixth Avenue. "Hot chocolate all around," he told the waitress. Louisa snuggled up against him, and he kissed the top of her head. "You both have to help me out. My stepmother has asked me to organize a birthday party for Sibyl."

"What do I do?" Louisa demanded.

"You select the crepe paper, Louisa; and you, Bliss, can tell me the names of her friends at school."

Bliss groaned. "I'd rather select the crepe paper."

"If that means it would be easier to invite the entire junior class, it will be done." He opened his notebook with its Columbia insignia and began to write. "One junior class. Two serving maids, three live musicians, and a man to tend the bar."

"Ask Colin Bragg. He needs a job."

"One Colin Bragg," he sang, "three French hens, two

79

calling birds and thirty-five Partridge Mellon girls with escorts." Putting down his pen he looked up at her. "Except for you, Blissful Joy. You're mine."

She was? The words sang. She had been invited to the ball by the prince. Every member of the junior class and Colin Bragg would be there to witness her triumph. She had misinformed Louisa. Life *was* a fairy tale.

13

Now there was a second test date circled in vermillion magic marker on Bliss's calendar. Sibyl's Birthday and the SATs. If she could do well on the SATs she would prove herself an academic success. If she could do well at the party, she would prove herself a social success. Bliss wanted to do very very well at both tests.

Sitting on her bed before going to school, she studied the calendar with growing apprehension. Sibyl's birthday was on the twenty-fifth of April. The SATs were the ninth of May. The relentless army of X's advanced closer and closer, stopping at that day, April 7. She had put a small blue dot on the date to remind herself of the conference she had that morning with Mrs. Bernside, Partridge Mellon's college adviser.

Mrs. Bernside's small office was in the basement of the building. There was a wooden bench outside the office upon which Bliss sat waiting. Each junior had a scheduled conference at which she would go over the college questionnaire she had filled out and receive a list of possible-choice schools Mrs. Bernside had drawn up. Bliss could hear the muffled voices of Mrs. Bernside and Susu Bennet through the door. She thought she heard the word "horse" and wondered if Susu was asking if she could take hers to college. When she came out, Susu passed her with a weepy nod.

"I hope *your* mother hasn't got her heart set on her alma mater for you," Mrs. Bernside said.

Bliss recalled that Mrs. Bennet was active in the Radcliffe Club. Susu's birthdays were celebrated in the club's dining room every fall.

"No. *I* am the one who has my heart set on my mother's alma mater."

Mrs. Bernside looked at Bliss's folder. "Certainly you should try for Vassar. I would say reach for it, but with your PSAT scores you'd be wise to give serious consideration to some of the schools on the list I've made up for you. I always say be realistic." She looked up and smiled brightly. "You've been an excellent student and I see you've worked in the History Club, but unless you pick up those scores in May you'd be asking for disappointment if you don't open your mind to other schools."

Bliss accepted the list without looking at it. Mrs. Bernside's telephone rang. "We'll talk again in the fall when you've studied the list and taken your SATs," she said as Bliss stood up to leave.

When she left the office Bliss went to the library for her free period. She wanted to peruse the list in peace. Sitting at the first long table was Jenny.

"I am dying of curiosity," she hissed. "What did you draw?"

Bliss ran her eye down the list. "Most of them, you never heard of."

"Try me. They're probably my dream school."

"I'd rather not."

"Bliss, are you kidding?"

"Do I look like I'm kidding? All these years of hard work and planning down the drain." She felt close to tears. "Just because of that test."

Mrs. Preston, the librarian, put a finger over her lips and said, "Shhhhhhh."

"Planning for what?" Jenny asked.

"Vassar."

"Why Vassar?"

Bliss shrugged.

"You don't know anything about it except that Polly went there and it's got prestige. You want a prestige school."

"That's not true."

"Sure it's true. It's true what everybody says about you, you are a shallow snob."

"Everybody says that about me?" Bliss reeled.

"Bernside would have laughed out loud if I said I wanted to apply to Vassar. Does that mean I've got a bargain-basement brain? It so happens I've worked hard myself. I just don't have very good grades to show for it."

"If you two have anything more to say to each other, why don't you step outside. The library is not the proper place to talk things out." Mrs. Preston stood at the end of their table, glaring.

Bliss picked up her book bag quickly and left the library. She had never seen Jenny so angry. She had never heard her lash out so cruelly. She knew the anger was the result of Jenny's uncontrollable jealousy. But as she stooped to the water fountain, she wondered if any of what Jenny had said was true. She *did* want a prestige school. She *did* want the world to know who she was. College? Ivy League, Vassar. Boy friend? Howard Oaks, Columbia. Those things made her somebody other than Dan and Polly's pathetic kid.

Jenny would have nothing to do with her for the rest of the day. As she walked by herself toward the subway, Bliss was joined by Susu. "Now I go home to face the music. Bernside says there is no way I can get into Radcliffe and Mummy's going to have to accept it."

"Did you want to go there?"

Susu shrugged. "Did I want Partridge Mellon? Mummy went to P.M. I wished I could have gone to a school with a good stable. Millbank, maybe." They trudged in silence. "I wish I was out from under all this. I wish I was on a horse farm. I'd train them and groom them and paint pictures of them."

When they went down into the subway, Susu joined the group she always sat with, and Bliss sat by herself to avoid them. Four seniors rushed in just before the door closed. They crowded into a few empty seats across from her.

"Waiting list at Bennington. What does that mean?"

"You heard already?"

"Lots of us have."

"Find out how far down on the waiting list you are."

Their voices were so shrill they carried over the train.

"Did you get Vassar?"

"I have to choose between it and Princeton, but I didn't hear from Princeton yet. I probably won't till next week. I may die first."

"*Pooooor youuuuu.*" The cry went up.

"Victoria got Yale."

"Victoria got everything."

"Darcy got Harvard. Partridge Mellon got three into

Harvard last year. Bronx Science got two. I don't remember what Dalton got."

Bliss shut her eyes tight. Why were they screaming? What did it mean? The gates of heaven had opened and a small band were chosen to pass through. The entry ticket was a score card, a connection, high school performance, a good last name, the right small town. If Jenny thought she was her only friend, she'd have to think again. Bliss decided to call Susu Bennet that evening.

As she came to the door at three-thirty, the telephone was ringing.

It was Delphi Pilpel. "I won't beat around the shrubs. I feel funny about the other night. Maybe I embarrassed you with your friends."

"It was okay," Bliss lied.

"I don't think so. You looked miserable. Last thing I want to do is make you upset with me."

"No, really."

"When you walk Blackball, stop by the office. I'll make tea."

"I don't know . . ."

"Great, see you around four."

A woman carrying a cat box, tears streaming down her cheeks, was leaving Delphi Pilpel's office as Bliss entered it. The receptionist poked her head round the door to the examining room. "Bliss Bowman?" She smiled.

Bliss nodded.

"Sit down; Doctor's just washing up."

Bliss took the seat on which she had first seen Colin. She resented Delphi's summons. Why should she become caught up in a stranger's hopeless crush? It was bizarre.

The next time the door to the examining room opened, it was Delphi who stepped through it. "I'm sorry to keep you waiting, and so grateful you came. I just put on some tea."

Bliss and Blackball followed her through the examining room into a smaller office in the back. It was crammed with metal files and two oversize swivel chairs. On top of a low desk was a gas ring with an about-to-whistle kettle on it. Delphi took a box of creme cookies out of the file as well as two mugs and a teabag. Bliss watched her carefully pour out the water, dip the bag, and open the cookies. She handed Bliss her mug and they sat down.

"I am direct I think what I did the other night was dumb."

"Why?"

"If I were you, sixteen, seventeen, with a nice young boy and his sister, bringing them home to my father's house, I would have been . . ." She paused to think of the word. ". . . mortified, by what happened."

"What happened?" Bliss felt her heart beat. She had not expected this.

"*I* happened. I came in, crashing, I think is the word for it. Pursuing your dad is *my* word for it. I didn't have the good sense to leave."

"I think everyone had a fine time."

"Then why did you look so unhappy? I kept seeing your sad little face in front of me the whole next day. It was awful. I thought, Delphi, you fool. You go after the father and make an enemy of the daughter. This is no good. I read enough fairy tales to know that."

"I don't think of you as my enemy," Bliss said earnestly.

Delphi smiled for the first time, her face transforming itself from plain to pretty. "You don't? Oh good. Because let me tell you something, Bliss. I would be very good for your father. He needs somebody mature and sensible who likes him a lot."

"You?"

"Me. Exactly. That Tree-Anna was nice, but it's silly for him to take up with girls like that. He's too old for such things and it tires him out. It's bad for his health and his, how do you say . . ." She tapped her forehead. ". . . his spirits. I told him so."

"You did?" Bliss said unbelievingly.

"Certainly. I explained to you I am very direct. I told him how good I would be for him."

"What did he say?"

For the first time Delphi looked a bit sly. She lowered her head. "He invited me to dinner so we could discuss my ideas further. I'm going up there tonight."

"Don't worry, I won't crash," Bliss laughed.

"Thanks — that was the next thing I was going to ask you."

Bliss finished her tea and set the mug down as the outside bell sounded.

"Ah, next patient." Delphi rubbed her hands on her white coat and stood up. "I hope we cleared the airs."

"We cleared the airs." Bliss went out the door Delphi held open for her.

"It's hopeless," Bliss spoke in the low voice she used to her dog when on the street. "She's got herself a hopeless passion, but we have to admire her persistence and honesty."

Blackball turned her head, flashing a look of incomprehension. "I didn't get that. I *am* a dog," she seemed to say.

14

Two more days passed, during which Jenny pretended not to see her. She wasn't obviously rude so that anyone else would notice, but she waited till Bliss had chosen a table for lunch and then made sure to sit as far away as the room would allow. She avoided Bliss's eye and turned her head so as to be sure not to meet it. The two days were a strain. Bliss went over their conversation in the library, feeling worse and worse about it. She had hurt Jenny. She had been so caught up in her own feelings that she had been insensitive to her friend's.

Lying on her bed with Blackball and Barron's, she could not concentrate. Her thoughts kept drifting back to the words they had exchanged in the library. It was four-thirty, the time she would usually call Jenny or go over to see her. She'd had enough of this argument. But as she reached for the phone in the kitchen, it rang.

"Who's Delphi Pilpel?" It was Polly from her office.

"I told you. She's the lady vet who's chasing Dan."

"Is she catching him?"

"Never. Dan has a new wood nymph. Pilpel is hopeless."

"I don't know about that," Polly said. "He's had dinner with her twice this week. When I called just now she picked up the phone. On my way back from lunch, I bumped into them. They were buying a lamp."

For the first time Bliss realized Polly was upset by Dan's private life. In the past she had been amused by it. She enjoyed consoling Dan when his girl of the moment left and commiserating with him when she stayed too long. Now that Dan had found a hopeless, plain, middle-aged woman, Polly was worried. Amazing. "Believe me, Polly, it's nothing. She's not Dan's type. He finds her convenient. He's using her. He said so. She was invited to dinner so that Blackball would get free medical care."

"I liked her," Polly said. "She looks serious. I think *it's* serious."

When she hung up, Bliss was overwhelmed with the desire to tell Jenny this piece of news. But the phone rang again. It was Colin.

"Polly's not home."

"I'm not calling Polly. I'm calling you."

"Why?"

"Thanks for suggesting me to Harold Oaks. He's engaged me for the big party. Will you be there?"

"Yes."

"Howard's going all out. I know what Sibyl means to him."

"He's very kind to her."

"Kind?" Colin sounded puzzled. "At any rate I want to thank you for that critique you gave me on *Private Lives*. It really helped. Did Polly tell you we did the scene for class?"

"She said it went well."

"She called it her farewell performance. But *I'm* working on a new scene. *Golden Boy*. Maybe you'd like to hear it sometime. I would be interested to know what you think."

"Would you?"

"Unless, uh, maybe a better idea would be a movie or dinner. We could do both." He sounded to her as if he were winding down, or drying up. He could dry up and turn to dust as far as she was concerned. Trying to score with Polly by making condescending small talk with her daughter was the limit. Next he'd bring her a box of lollipops and a coloring book. "Wait till he sees me at that party," she thought.

After he had said good-bye twice and hung up, Bliss put on her coat. Fight or no fight, she was going over to Jenny's. She had too much to keep to herself or tell on the phone.

"I'm sort of busy," Jenny said over the building intercom. "I'm in the middle of clocking myself on the math, but you can come up anyway."

Leaning in her doorway as Bliss emerged from the elevator Jenny gave her an icy gaze.

"I'm sorry about what happened in the library," Bliss said.

"That's a good beginning." Jenny stepped aside and let her in. Bliss walked behind her into the bedroom. The all too familiar Barron's was spread open on the bed, a sharp number two pencil laid diagonally across the open page.

"I thought about your evaluation of me and I agree with you. I *am* interested in prestige. I am a snob. I do want status. I don't think I have to tell you why."

"Those were good insights," Jenny acknowledged.

"Well expressed, too. But laying it out doesn't make you terrific." She closed the Barron's and sat on the edge of her bed.

"I thought it would help," Bliss said in a whisper. "I really don't want to have to shape Susu Bennet up as your replacement. What else can I do?"

Suddenly Jenny grinned. "Oh forget it."

Bliss collapsed with relief on the bean bag. "Let me tell you what's been happening." When she had finished her report on the two telephone calls, there was silence.

"What's your prognosis?" Jenny said after a while.

"Polly is scared. Middle age and fears of mortality have been transferred to fear of Dan's forming a serious relationship with Delphi. Polly is distracting herself as usual. Colin is attempting to use me to get to Polly. 'Put in a good word for me with your mother, little girl.' He thinks he can manipulate me."

Jenny nibbled on her pencil and frowned.

"Well?" Bliss said impatiently.

"I'm afraid to tell you what I think."

"Why?"

"Because I don't agree with you."

"Is this the first time you haven't agreed with me lately? Am I supposed to fall apart?" Bliss did not care for the sound of her own voice.

"No," Jenny was very serious. "It's true we haven't been agreeing lately. It's also true we haven't been great friends."

"Whatever it is you have to say, I really think I can take it." She was beginning to feel prickly and hot in spite of herself. "Try me."

"What if I told you that I think Polly knows it's serious between Dan and Delphi, that Colin is as interested in

91

you as you are in him, and that you are so full of defenses and pretenses you don't let yourself see the truth of anything anymore, including who you are."

"I'd say you're crazy."

"Then I'm crazy." Jenny shrugged. "Remember we once agreed to be honest with each other and not to use psychology to cover up what we didn't want to confront, but to unearth the true nature of our actions no matter how painful?"

"Then to be painfully honest with you, Jennifer Sewel, you are taking advantage of our friendship and of my confidence and trust in you to hurt me."

"What friendship? What confidence and trust?" Jenny looked bleak. "I used to think we had those things. Now all you give me are positions. You've changed, Bowman."

"How can I change, if you say I don't know who I am?"

Jenny narrowed her sad eyes. "You made yourself up. You decided to be a person who was NOT like Polly and Dan. I think you're a lot more like them than you think and it's driving you nuts."

"Nuts?"

"Well, nasty. You always came on as Miss Solid Sensible Practical Down-to-Earth Bliss. In fact you're as daydreamy, impulsive, and romantic as Polly and Dan together."

"Oh shut up." Bliss got up so quickly her elbow knocked down one of the bottles on Jenny's dresser.

"All this stuff with the dog. You think you'd have gotten into it if you were the Blissful Joy you pretend to be?"

Bliss was already out of Jenny's room, rushing down the hall toward the front door. "I don't see why I should leave myself open to this sort of scene again. I will definitely put some effort into Susu Bennet. And don't get me wrong, it's *not* that I'm angry or hurt — it's that I'm mature enough to realize when I've outgrown a relationship." She didn't turn to look at Jenny before she slammed the front door. Her eyes were stinging with tears of rage and disappointment. They were her own affair.

As she let herself into the apartment the phone was ringing. For a wonderful moment Bliss thought it might be Jenny calling to take back everything she had said.

"I'm ringing up to keep you posted with my up-to-the-minute news bulletins."

"Who is this?"

"Delphi, of course."

"You don't have to keep me posted, Delphi."

"But I want to. Firstly, the dinner was terrific. I think he's seeing the light. He asked me to the theater the next night and dinner too. Also he wanted me to help him pick out some things for his living room. That's a good sign, isn't it?"

"I honestly don't know," Bliss said, exasperated. "And I'm not sure that it's a good idea for you to confide in me and ask my advice about your relationship with Dan."

There was a pause which on the telephone seemed very long. Then Delphi drew in her breath. "I didn't mean to do an upsetting thing," she said. "I told you how I feel. I will be good for your father."

"But what if it doesn't work out, Delphi? What if you get your hopes up and Dan is just, you know . . ."

"Playing around with me? Humoring me? Getting free shots for Blackball and a lot of flattering goo-goo eyes from old cross-eyes? I thought of all that. Believe me. Remember, I told you I never got anything easy." She laughed. "I wasn't clever or pretty. I had to work hard for what I won, but that's okay. I'm good at losing. Not sensitive. Very practical. People like you and Dan need people like me."

"*Me* and Dan?"

"Sure, you and your father, dreamy, romantic types. You could both use a Delphi Pilpel. Believe me, I would balance the act."

"I'm not like Dan."

"Not like Dan?" Delphi giggled. "Who finds dogs on subways and keeps them?"

This *is* a gang up, Bliss thought miserably. And I am not paranoid.

15

It was awkward not having a friend. There was no one to compare case histories with. There was no one to eat lunch with, or get homework from. Bliss found herself making a fact out of her threat to Jenny. She was working Susu Bennet up for the vacant spot. She had given Sibyl a try, but Sibyl was too unreliable and eccentric. Susu, on the other hand, was dependable and loyal. It was a pity, they both agreed, that Bliss had no interest in horses and Susu had no interest in psychology.

"*I do* love your drawings though," Bliss said at lunch. She had been going through a heap of Susu's new horse sketches. "You're terrifically talented."

"Not really." Susu bent her head.

"You have a problem handling praise."

"Well, I think I'm good at drawing pictures of horses, but it's nothing like being able to figure out people's unconscious motives."

Every time Bliss used a word of psychological jargon,

Susu's face lit up with reverence. They were full of uneasy flattery and praise of one another.

Nina Sarton banged her tray across the table from Bliss and sat down wearily.

"You look awful," Susu remarked.

"Another sleepless night. We're all insomniacs in our house. I collided with my mom at three A.M."

"I don't have that problem," Susu said. "I think of my horse and a field and a summer morning and I am asleep."

Nina opened her milk container. "I think, horse is to field as lion is to jungle as bird is to cage as ant is to bee."

"Is that the price you pay for those high scores?" Susu laughed.

"It certainly helps if you don't have an imagination," Nina said matter-of-factly. "The schools want people with my kind of head."

"You're always putting yourself down."

"All I'm saying is that it's easier to focus on *their* landscape if you don't have one of your own."

"Accept the fact that you're good at those tests and enjoy it."

"Why? So that one day when I'm recalling the great future behind me, and pass a gallery showing your horse paintings, I'll feel worse? No thanks. I'll cash in on my brain and go to law school."

"You can be my lawyer," Bliss said.

"You can be my psychologist."

"I hope neither of us needs each other."

Across the room, Bliss saw that Jenny was sitting with Francesca and Sibyl. Perhaps it was a stroke of luck that they had quarreled. She would never have had anything to do with Susu and Nina otherwise.

96

"Have you got a dress for Sib's party yet?" Susu was asking.

"We are not about to have the what-are-you-wearing-to-the-bash conversation again." Nina threw up her hands.

"It will be very posh." Susu could not be stopped. "Francesca says the Oakses are the last word in chic. She says they're having a bar man and a live combo and maybe some stars from the Oaks stage productions. Francesca's parents visited Sib's parents last year. They told her the Oakses make divine parties."

"But it's the brother who's making the party." Nina reached into her school bag and pulled out the frayed pink and orange striped invitation every girl in the class had received. "Look, it says, 'RSVP, Howard Oaks.'" Then slowly turning her head she focused on Bliss. "He's the one Sib says is crazy about you."

Bliss nodded demurely, enjoying the moment more than she would ever admit.

"God, we're sitting here with a celebrity and we nearly forgot," Susu cried. "Tell us — do we get the Rolling Stones? What are you wearing? What's it like to catch an Oak?"

"Fell an Oak," Nina corrected.

"He's very nice," Bliss said in Polly's queenly tone. "Uncomplicated and sweet."

"That's not what Francesca said," Nina bore down.

"This is almost as interesting as horses." Susu clapped her hands. "What did Francesca say?"

Nina bent toward them. "She said that Mrs. Oaks was dying for him to go out of town to college, but he refused. He was accepted to Dartmouth and MIT, but chose Columbia so he could stay home."

"Bizarre," Susu exclaimed.

"Mrs. Oaks doesn't want him influencing Sibyl." Nina challenged Bliss with this as if they were already in a court of law. "Is all this garbage, or is it true?"

Bliss changed her mind. She wished she was back sitting with Jenny, fight or no fight. "He seems to be a very stable person. He treats Sibyl with compassion and a keen awareness of her psychological needs."

"Isn't psychology wonderful," Susu said. Mercifully the bell rang. Lunch was at an end. Bliss had had enough of Susu and Nina for one day.

"I had enough of them for one day," she confided to Blackball later. They were sharing a snack in the kitchen. Rye Krisp and cheese with milk. "I'm starting to eat like a dog," Bliss said. "Now with luck maybe I'll contract your state of mind, peace and tranquillity." But when the snack was consumed she was still restless. The apartment seemed small and grim. She couldn't start her homework, wouldn't call Susu, and was determined not to phone Jenny. Polly wouldn't be home for hours. She turned on the radio. One sweep of the dial brought hysterical continuous news and a fund-raising marathon. The television set offered soaps, which reminded her depressingly of Dan and Trianna. She began to pace with Blackball in her wake.

"We have got to get out of here," Bliss said out loud. "Let's go."

On the street, a raw wind had come up from the river. It smelled of the water and seemed to carry them toward Washington Square. They walked quickly, sometimes breaking into a jog together. There were no chess players at the concrete tables and no strollers or loungers on the benches or under the arch. People hurried to get out of the weather. A few dog walkers stamped their feet and blew on their hands, waiting impatiently while their animals sniffed among the soggy leaves of past summers. When Bliss noticed five dogs together, she had a fairly good idea of who held their leashes.

"Every time I come here, I hope to see you," Colin said. "Today I've been lucky."

"You must be taking a course in gallantry."

His pale face colored and he looked abashed. "Look, Bliss, I'd really like to talk to you. This isn't the place. Can we go somewhere warm and sit down?"

"With six dogs? Are you kidding?"

"Can I walk you home?"

She shrugged and turned away. "Polly won't be back from work."

"What does that have to do with it?"

"I thought you ought to know."

"It isn't Polly I want to see, it's you. It's you I keep making blunders with, not Polly."

"What sort of blunders?" They began to walk together in the direction of Bliss's building.

"I call you up because I want to see you and, like an egotistical ass, ask you to watch me perform a scene from *Golden Boy*. Then I torment you about your dog. I taunt you about going to Partridge Mellon. I even intrude myself on your relationship with your mother. I've been awful to you and I want to apologize." When she didn't respond, except by lowering her head, he went on. "The only way I can explain what I've done is that I've seen myself in you. I've argued with myself through you."

"I don't understand." Bliss stopped walking to face him.

"When I blamed you for wanting the Partridge Mellon prestige I was accusing my old self through you. I wanted Princeton because of what it stood for. Going there made

99

my family proud and happy, my school proud and happy, and me proud and happy. When I got there I found I was certainly not happy, that that kind of pride is meaningless. I discovered the work that was really important to me. I knew what I wanted to do but I was terrified to leave. To be without an affiliation that gave me status was frightening. Even though I knew what I wanted, I dreaded leaving the safe shelter."

"But I don't know what I want," Bliss said. "I haven't found the work that's important to me."

"That's why I'm apologizing. I was unfair. The theater means everything to me. Getting better at what I do, working at it, feeling myself grow, has taken the place of needing that association with prestige."

In spite of herself, Bliss liked what he said. She found it exciting. She was entranced by his lean, fervent face. For a moment she wished to believe he was telling her these things because of herself and not to have them relayed back to Polly.

"I hope one day what has happened to me will happen to you," he said. "Then you'll know what has true meaning for you and what is pretense. It will be easier to differentiate."

It was beginning to grow dark. They walked to Bliss's stoop. When she looked up she saw that the light was on in the living room. Her enthusiasm for Colin ebbed. "I can't ask you up just now."

"No. I never . . . I mean the dogs . . . I just wanted to explain. Sometime I'd like to see you."

"Why not." She didn't enjoy watching someone else stammer. She pulled Blackball up the stairs after her. If she had left the house confused and distressed, she was returning to it a hundred times more so.

* * *

When she got upstairs, Bliss found Polly home from work. She was very animated, her face flushed with some secret excitement.

"Do you want to buy a new dress for that party or wear something of mine?" Polly stooped to place a foil-lined paper bag containing their chicken dinner on the middle rack of the oven. "I think you might look beautiful in my black Mexican wedding dress." She turned the oven on for the chicken and put a bottle of white wine on the table.

"What's the wine for, Pol?"

"Celebration."

"Tell me."

"In a minute." She twisted a corkscrew into the cork and pulled till her face was red. Bliss set the table and put out two wineglasses. She opened the plastic containers of cucumber salad and macaroni.

"I think the paper bag is burning."

"I wish I had a stove I could trust." Polly took the smoldering bag out of the oven. "I can't even do good take-out food." She slipped the bird onto a plate and poured out the wine. "They've asked me to take a permanent job at the agency."

"That's wonderful."

"You said it."

"Now that I said it," Bliss reconsidered, "I wonder why. What happened to the theater?"

"It wasn't working out. You tried to tell me that."

"But you loved it."

"But I wasn't good enough. I *am* good at my agency job. I'll get better."

Realizing that her reaction was wrong and not understanding why herself, Bliss forced a smile and kept it on her lips while Polly cut up the chicken and spooned out the salads. As Polly lifted her glass, Bliss felt her heart sink. "Here's to a new and wonderful beginning, Blissful."

Watch out what you wish for, Jenny had said. Why did she feel so awful about Polly's good news? Was it true that she didn't understand herself at all? She wished she could call Jenny, but that was the last thing she would let herself do.

After dinner Bliss tried on Polly's dress. The tiers of tucked cotton and lace swirled to her ankles. The square neck framed her white throat and her face. "You look so beautiful," Polly said. "I wish you were going on the stage. I'd like people to see my little girl on the home screen."

"You shouldn't say things like that to me. I may get the impression that you're using me to relive your youth."

Polly began to scowl. Bliss giggled and turned on her heel. "They'll call me the dancing therapist. You could get me dates at analytic conventions."

"You're being fresh!" Polly was amazed. "You're actually joking around! You've gone and changed on me."

"Look who's talking about change."

"That reminds me." Polly sobered. "Dan called at the office. There's something he wants to tell you. He'd like you to have dinner at his place tomorrow night."

Suddenly Bliss was cold. "What is it about?"

"Maybe he's taking a job in a bank," Polly quipped in her stagy "light tone." "Even if I knew I wouldn't want to steal his thunder."

Thunder? Bliss took off the dress and went back to her room. The weather in her world was changing. There was no question about it.

* * *

The following evening, when she arrived at Dan's she found him with Delphi in the kitchen. Delphi was arranging a little tray with three glasses and a dish of nuts and sliced cheese. Dan was breaking ice out of the freezer to fill a bucket in which to set a bottle of champagne. They carried all this into the living room. Dan and Delphi giggled. Dan put his arm around Delphi's waist. Delphi kissed Dan's cheek. Dan kissed Delphi's nose. Bliss sat down. Delphi slipped Bliss a happy intimate wink.

She felt as if she were watching a slide projector show on a stranger's living room. *Click.* Dan opening the champagne. *Click.* Delphi applauding and laughing. *Click.* The glasses being filled. *Click.* Champagne bubbling over onto the carpet. *Click.* The lifted glass. The announcement. "We will get married in May." Hugs. Kisses. Sips. Clinks.

Dan went back into the kitchen to start the steaks.

Delphi took Bliss's hand. "Perhaps you are shocked," she said gently. "I told you, I work hard for what I want. I'm crazy about your father." She kissed Bliss on the cheek and stood up. "It shows you what a person can do in spite of all the drawbacks."

The rest of the evening played before Bliss in the same detached way. She felt cut off from the action and unable to respond to it. She had to remind herself to speak, smile, and react. Delphi and Dan would marry in Dan's apartment. There would be a small reception. There would be no honeymoon. Dan planned to work in a stock company in Connecticut during the summer and they would take a house. Bliss would join them (they hoped) for a few weeks in the country. In the fall they would live in Dan's apartment.

They sat at the table in the living room while Dan served up steaks in garlic and vinegar, salad and herbed bread, telling her their news, holding hands, laughing and awaiting her response.

"If it hadn't been for you, none of this would have happened," Dan said.

"You mean if it hadn't been for Blackball," Bliss reminded him.

"You mean I have a dog to thank for changing my life?" said Delphi.

"We all do," said Bliss.

Delphi went to make coffee and fetch dessert.

"I suppose I've really shocked you, Blissful," Dan said gently.

"No, no, no," she protested quickly.

"Yes, yes, yes. It's all over your face. You're no actress, sweetheart."

"Sorry."

"Don't be sorry. I'm a bit in shock myself. I never thought anything like this would happen to me. Delphi Pilpel. My God. But she's terrific. She makes my life work. She's actually fantastic. Organized, loving. She took my papers and filed them. Found three checks I forgot to cash, under the sofa. Made a list of agents. Sent out my résumé. Got me a new manager. Balanced my checkbook. There's no reason for my checks to bounce. I had the money; it was just . . ." He shrugged.

"Under the sofa."

"Yes." He looked baffled. "How did you know? Oh sweetie." He got up to hug her. "I feel as if the curtain's going up on a brand-new show now. At first I thought she was sort of plain and peculiar. But the woman is a real sleeper. She grows on you. Adorable, funny, charming."

"And she makes your life work," Bliss repeated dully.

Delphi returned with a tray of coffee cups and a pecan pie.

"I was just telling my daughter how crazy I am for you, Delph."

"Then keep talking, please."

Dan kept talking, Delphi poured coffee, and Bliss knew with certainty that for the rest of her life she would have a hard time eating pecan pie.

"What was the mysterious announcement?" Polly was waiting for Bliss as she came in the door.

"Dan's getting married."

"I thought so. Dr. Pilpel meant business. She even called me to introduce herself and tell me what a nice daughter I have."

"I never expected it."

"Even though I did, it seems strange," Polly admitted. She reached out and took Bliss's hand.

"I thought I had worked all this stuff out years ago."

Every Child's Book on Divorce.

Bliss nodded, "I went through all the chapters and marked off all the stages. One, Two, Three, I put them behind me."

"Unfortunately real-life events don't occur as neatly as chapters. It's good to find that out. I still am."

In her room Bliss fell on the bed. Blackball jumped up on her pillow. Bliss began to laugh, but her eyes blurred and she put her face into Blackball's neck. Soon the fur was damp. Blackball licked her nose, whimpering sympathy. Bliss opened the SAT review to a random page. Her eye fell upon a question. She read it. She reread it. She had to choose from four misleading answers the one that was least misleading. A batting sensation filled her chest. It was as if a panicked bird were beating its wings inside her ribs. Trapped. She couldn't understand anything. Dan and his marriage, Polly and her job, Howard Oaks and herself, Colin Bragg and Polly, Jenny and why they were no longer friends. None of her old systems was working and worst of all she had nothing to take their place. She got ready for bed and fell immediately to sleep. But her dreams were troubling. She was wearing the black wedding dress. Everyone at Sibyl's party was exclaiming over how beautiful she looked. Howard Oaks wanted to dance with her, but Colin was angry. She couldn't catch his eye. Louisa Knight was demanding she return her mother. "You lost her," Louisa cried. Bliss was looking frantically under the seats of a darkened subway car crying, "I'll find her, I'll find her."

"Watch out what you wish for," Jenny was saying on a loudspeaker.

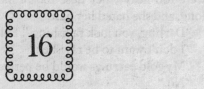

16

For the next two weeks, the subject that dominated all conversation among the members of the junior class at Partridge Mellon was the surprise seventeenth birthday party for Sibyl Oaks. These conversations had to be conducted in whispers with an eye out for Sibyl herself. Bliss spent almost as much time daydreaming about the party as studying Barron's.

"One scarcely knows what to wear," Francesca complained to Bliss in the locker room. "One doesn't want to look tacky. Of course *you* can wear anything you like. *You* seem to be some sort of hostess."

Bliss knew that what she was really saying was, how did an outsider sneak under the ropes? And now that you're under do I need to pay attention to you? She rather enjoyed watching Francesca in her muddle.

On the evening of the party Bliss was nearly sick with nerves. She took a hot bath, but her hands and feet were freezing. She put on rouge and couldn't get her cheeks to match. She looked out the window at a driving cold April rain and knew her shoes would be ruined. Her brows were too heavy, her nose too pronounced, her neck too long, and she hated her hair.

"Darling, you look ravishing," Polly said.

"I don't want to be ravished."

"My gold earrings would be perfect."

"No."

But Polly was in her bedroom rummaging around in the mess she called her notions drawer. "Here we go." The earrings were heavy gold hoops that dangled almost to the line of the jaw. Bliss's reflection told her that Polly had been right. Suddenly she looked beautiful.

Howard phoned. "I'm running late. We had an awful time getting Sib out of the house. Her mother took her to a matinee. At the last minute she decided she didn't want to go. We had to talk her into it. Could you get yourself up here? I need help with the decorations. At any rate you could get Louisa out of my hair."

When she arrived at the apartment Bliss found Howard and Louisa in the dining room trying to arrange a center-piece that had dozens of crepe paper streamers attached to it.

"Hullo," Howard said. "Deal with this. I have to get Louisa started on the balloons. You'll need a step ladder to attach the streamers." He glanced at her dress. "I hope your long skirt won't get in the way."

"My long black Mexican wedding dress in which I look ravishing," Bliss muttered to herself as he dashed off.

"You look so *old*," Louisa called over her shoulder.

The dress did get in her way. She had to hold it up so as not to trip on the ladder. She couldn't position the streamers as he wanted them. It was difficult to make em stick to the wall sconces. Her earrings kept snagging in her hair.

Howard came back into the room. "No, not that way. ou've got them too far apart. I told you I wanted the fect of an inverted tent."

"You didn't tell me."

"He told me," said the glum maid who was setting up a uffet table. "I didn't know what he was talking about."

Bliss undid the streamers she had attached. The doorell started to ring. She could hear the bustle of arriving uests being ushered through the gallery. There was ughter. Sounds of ice in glasses came from the library. he wondered with a pang if Colin had arrived.

"Did you finish?" Howard poked his head in. "By the ay, you look very sweet."

"Sweet?"

She climbed down from the step ladder and went into he library. A bar had been set up. Louisa, her cheeks ushed with excitement, was presenting each new guest ith a candle to be lit when Sibyl walked in the door. unches of balloons bobbed on the ceiling.

Jenny came in with a tall stooped young man; she oked through Bliss and talked to Howard, "This is harlie Frobish." Then to Bliss: "Nice dress. Charlie, eet Blissful Joy Bowman."

"You look beautiful, Bliss," Susu gushed. "Like a inting."

"I hope not one of yours," Jenny said.

Francesca hurried through the door. "We saw them epping out of a taxi as the elevator closed. They're on eir way up."

An expectant hush fell over the room. Tina Block giged. Ellie Davis pinched her. Mary Roundtree hiccuped. hree musicians in the living room tuned their instru-

109

ments. Howard dimmed the lights. The door opened

In the dark, music and voices took a moment to finc each other, but as they began to converge in a grouf toward the library, and the spots of candlelight cas rounds of light on their faces, both voices and instru ments gained confidence.

"Happy birthday, dear Sibyl, happy birthday to you."

In the flickering light, Sibyl's eyes flashed. She steppec backward; leaving Mrs. Oaks stranded in the middle o the circle. "But it's for YOU, darling," Mrs. Oaks said.

Howard dropped Bliss's hand. The glance he and hi stepsister exchanged was both intimate and knowing.

"Dirty trick," Sibyl growled. "I haven't a thing tc wear."

"There's a dress on your bed," said Mrs. Oaks with strained giggle.

Everyone laughed. The music got louder. Guest moved back to the library and living room. Mrs. Oak took off her coat. Sibyl threw her jacket over one shoul der. "You've heard of Cinderella, Howie, just watch this." She skipped down the corridor toward her room.

"The afternoon went off without a hitch," Mrs. Oak said to Howard. "For a while I thought she suspected. Sh said she wanted to come home after the theater. But whe I mentioned tea at the Palm Court she changed her mind You know what a thing she has for that place." Mr. Oaks's constantly shifting eyes narrowed on the ba "Why is Mrs. McAddam at the bar? I thought you hired man."

"I thought so too."

"You can't depend on anyone anymore, no matte what you pay. Is Lyman here? He said he'd be a littl late." She set off on her wobbly heels, preoccupied an apprehensive. "I'm so glad it stopped raining."

110

Couples had begun to dance in a part of the living room where a rug had been removed. Howard went to the library and brought back glasses of punch for himself and Bliss. They drank in silence. The music was too loud to speak over. After a while Howard led her into the living room and they began to dance. At least they squeezed into a space on the living room floor and shuffled back and forth. Jenny and Charlie Frobish were shifting around just behind them. "Sorry," Bliss said when she knocked Jenny's arm with her elbow.

"Funny, you don't look it."

Howard kept his eyes over her shoulder. "It doesn't usually take her so long to dress," he said. "Would you do me a favor and check on Sib?"

Bliss pushed past the knot of dancers, down a carpeted hall which led to Sibyl's room. The door was open. On the bed was a jumble of clothing. "Sibyl?" Bliss called, knowing that she was gone. "Sibyl?" She caught her own reflection in the mirrored dresser. She looked miserable and bereft. "Cinderella in reverse. I was a princess *before* I got to the ball. Now if I could only find my pumpkin, I'd clear out."

In the kitchen she met Howard. "Not there."

The maid, who Bliss remembered from her previous visit, turned from the sink. "She left by the kitchen door. I said, 'Miss Sib, is that you?' and she ran out. She went down the back stairs. I thought it was some joke."

Mrs. Oaks came in from the dining room. "We're out of ice, Jessie — I told you to bring some."

Howard took her elbow. "Sibyl's run off."

"No, she went to change."

"Jessie saw her leave."

Mrs. Oaks slammed her fist on the counter. "I knew this was a rotten idea."

Howard dashed to the back door.

"Where do you think you're going?"

"I'm going to find her."

"She'll come home by herself."

"Did my mother come home by herself?"

"That is a very insensitive thing to say to me considering that Sibyl is my only daughter."

"I wasn't thinking about your feelings. The only two people I ever cared about are gone."

"This is better than a television soap," Jessie observed happily to Bliss.

"You've admitted it," Mrs. Oaks said with satisfaction. "I told your father from the beginning that something was going on between you two. He said I was ridiculous. I told him that was why you chose Columbia, so you could stay here, stay with Sibyl. Nobody pays any attention to me. I'm supposed to be stupid. But I knew. I've always known. That's why Sibyl's been sick. You've made her sick." Mrs. Oaks's manner was distracted and complaining, but Howard was growing truly wild.

"There he goes!" Jessie crowed, as he ran out the door and down the steps. "Oh Lord."

Mrs. Oaks followed him onto the landing. "Damn you," she called.

The louvered doors from the gallery parted and Colin Bragg stepped through. "Sorry to be late," he said in his best Affected American. "I'm the bar man."

"A bar man," Mrs. Oaks wailed. "What do we do with a bar man, when we've lost the party."

"Miss Sibyl's run off and Mr. Howard's gone to find her," Jessie explained in the tone one would use to describe the plot of an opera.

"It won't be hard," said Colin. "There is a skinny girl crying on the lobby sofa, more or less waiting for someone to find her." He removed his coat and stood before them, resplendent in a rented tux.

"How do we explain about Sibyl?" Mrs. Oaks wondered. "Until they come back?"

"Wait till someone notices." He winked at Bliss. "Having a good time?"

"Super," she nodded violently.

They went into the library, where Colin relieved Mrs. McAddam of her duties. He checked the levels of his ice and punch and mixers. Mrs. Oaks went to "fix her face." Bliss wondered what to do that would make her look as if she were having the time of her life. She decided it would be best to keep moving about. She could pretend to have just been dancing, or looking for a friend, or returning from the bar. She saw Jenny staring at her over Charlie Frobish's shoulder. Jenny winked. Then her brows rose in a question. Bliss turned away as if she were searching for someone in particular. After a moment of this she ventured back to the library. Maybe Colin would think she had been dancing.

"What a wonderful party," Francesca said in the doorway.

"Yes, wonderful."

Colin was busy making martinis for Mr. and Mrs. Oaks. He shook the beaker as if he were a flamenco dancer. "When we were at Lakeville," he was saying over the din of music, "everybody knew Howard had a crush on his stepsister. He kept a photo of her in his locker. It was all terrifically romantic. Something out of a movie or a play." He deftly poured the martinis into glasses and added little onions.

"A movie or play in which I would have the role of nasty stepmother," Mrs. Oaks said. "It's not a role I would have chosen."

113

Before she could stop herself, Bliss's humiliation and distress turned to anger. She marched into their group. "How can you make light of it?" she demanded.

Three startled faces turned to face her.

"Howard and Sib aren't characters in a play. They're real. What happened tonight has to do with real people using each other and making up feelings to cover other feelings."

Mrs. Oaks drew back, frowning with distaste. She was about to say something when someone called out, "Sib, where have you been?"

"They're back." Mrs. Oaks ran off as fast as her heels would allow.

Bliss's sudden outburst fizzled. She was mortified. In the hubbub of Sibyl's return she headed for the coatrack. With blurred eyes and clumsy hands she shuffled among the jammed in coats and capes. The entire rack looked as if it was about to collapse. The beat of music in the living room changed to a ballad from one of the shows Polly loved to listen to.

"I'm risking my job for a dance." Colin appeared on the other side of a velvet cape.

"I want to go home." Bliss shook her head as she stepped into his arms. "Can you leave the bar?"

"I can leave entirely." He danced her away from the coatrack toward the end of the corridor. He danced as he acted, with grace and confidence. "It's a pity that a girl as lovely as you are should also be so pigheaded, judgmental, and narrow. I honestly don't know how Polly has put up with you."

"Polly put up with me?" Bliss cried. "Did it ever occur to you that I have had to deal with HER?"

"Deal with her how?"

"With her childishness, her dreams, her romances."

She grew bold. "Her crushes on men half her age. You think that's been easy?"

They stopped dancing, but continued to hold one another, almost as adversaries. His face above hers was intense. His expression amazed. "Polly knew how I felt about you," he said slowly, "and she was kind."

Bliss was speechless.

"Oh, Bliss." He shook his head sadly. "What a shabby little soul you have." He let go of her waist and her hand, and with a formal bow returned to his duties at the bar.

This time no one stopped Bliss from collecting her coat. No one intercepted her to remark on what a fantastic party it was. No one noticed her leave.

17

"*Why are you home so early?*" *Polly said, coming out of* her bedroom. "I would have thought you'd have danced all night." She stopped in her tracks. "Oh God, what happened?"

The crying Bliss had held back for hours broke like a wave on Polly's shoulder.

For a while Polly said lots of there there's and now now's. Then she settled Bliss on the sofa and went to fetch a glass of water. "Crying is therapy. I'm sure you know that if we all did it on regular schedules we'd eliminate acne and tooth decay."

Each time Bliss wound down to a few rib-wrenching sobs, humiliation and guilt would overwhelm her again.

Polly made tea. Bliss took deep breaths. "Colin told me I have a shabby soul."

"He's very theatrical. That must be a line out of a play he's rehearsing."

"I thought I knew things. I thought I understood things."

"What things?"

"About you and Dan, about myself, about Howard liking me, about the kind of person I am." Her eyes began to gush again. "I thought I had everything under control."

"I think we mixed you up," Polly decided. "After years of reckless, irresponsible behavior, Dan gets a good woman and I get a job. We pulled the rug out from under you. Is there anything else?"

"I thought you were involved with Colin."

"Involved with Colin?" Polly's eyes grew round. "He's only a boy. He told me he liked *you*. That's why I had him to dinner. Oh Bliss dear, did that all come out to-night?"

Bliss nodded. "And other things. Sibyl ran off and Howard went to get her. He said she was one of the two people he cared about."

"Maybe the other one was you."

Bliss shook her head. "His mother. And that little sister of his keeps insisting I find her mother because I found her dog, and Jenny tried to tell me the truth and we had a fight, and I was going to show everybody at Partridge Mellon who I am, and who I am is an idiot. I can't even take those tests."

"Who you are," said Polly softly, "is someone who can see painful things about herself."

"I don't know what you mean."

Polly took a deep breath and sat up straight. "I mean you can look at yourself and see what dumb things you've done and suffer for it and change because of it and grow out of it and fall on your face and get up again. If you learn how to do those things, the PSTUPIDs are unimportant."

Bliss listened without hearing. She was very tired. "I don't know if crying is good for acne and tooth decay, but it makes you very tired."

She slept without dreaming.

Monday morning Bliss didn't want to go to school. "They'll laugh at me. Francesca will want her pound of flesh."

"You'll only have to confront them on Tuesday," Polly reminded her. "Might as well get it over with."

More confrontations.

Bliss spent the day avoiding people. Jenny tried to say something to her but she pretended not to hear. She counted off the minutes on her watch. Finally it was time for the trip home. It had been her longest day at Partridge Mellon.

When at last she took her favorite seat on the downtown IRT local, relief engulfed her. Every muscle relaxed. She sat back and gazed mindlessly at the graffiti.

"Can I sit with you?" Susu asked.

Bliss shrugged.

"You looked so beautiful at the party. What happened? Why did you leave before we sang Happy Birthday?"

Nina Sarton sat down on the other side of her and Francesca and Julie hung from straps over her head. She was surrounded.

"You didn't miss much. Sib and her stepbrother came out of the closet. Is that incest?"

"No. They aren't related."

"I thought you were with him, Bliss."

"So did I. But it turns out, I was a cover."

"I missed it all," said Francesca. "Ate too much, drank too much, and got sick."

"The mother's a hoot."

"Took off her shoes and did a Lindy."

"No wonder Sib's so strange."

"It hasn't affected her brain. She got seven fifty in the verbal."

"I heard even higher than that. She's a genius."

"I got four fifty," said Bliss so suddenly that she even surprised herself. "I do very badly in those things. I think I'll sign up at Kooper's Kram School."

After a pause Francesca said, "I'll see you there. I got four ten. I hear that people who've taken their course go up as much as two hundred points."

"Kooper's is good," Susu said, "but it's on the other side of town. Why don't you try Miss McFee's with me, Bliss? She's on the West Side. There are four of us from P.M. already. We've only got two weeks till the test, so it's intense. Three hours, four times a week. She's tough but I like her. She says the SAT thing is a ripoff. A new American industry. Did you know that choosing a freshman class by SAT scores is only twelve percent better than random choice?"

"You mean if they picked our names out of a hat they'd be guessing nearly as well?"

"Except that all those people who work at the ATP in Princeton would be out of a job."

"No, they could start something called the HATs," Nina said. "Each testing center would feature an enormous hat. We'd all throw our names in."

"No one would accept that," said Julie. "It's too human. How could you ever computerize it?"

119

"Easy," Nina said. "You put square holes in the hat, seal it in plastic, and station two of those pompous gorgons from the ERB at its side."

They had been shrieking over the train's roar, so that when it pulled into a stop, their voices and laughter made heads turn. Bliss felt as if a weight had been lifted off her chest. The more she laughed, the lighter she felt. She didn't care who stared. A woman came through the door, just as it was about to close. She looked around the car and shuffled over to the place where Bliss would ordinarily have settled, in the corner, alone, determined not to associate with these girls. Determined to "show them." The car was nearly empty except for a few midday shoppers and students from half-day schools. The woman folded into her corner seat, between an assortment of shopping bags. She bent to check her possessions. Her fine ochre-colored hair fell like a screen over the side of her narrow pale face. Hair like Louisa's hair, clean and scraggly.

Her head bobbed with the motion of the train and her mouth moved in conversation with herself. Howard's mouth. "All I can tell you about it is it got on at Eighty-sixth Street," she had said. "I never talk to strangers. My advice to you is, don't get involved." For Bliss it was as if a curtain had parted. The woman stood up to leave.

"Where are you going, Bowman?" Francesca said. "It's not Christopher Street."

"I'm going to get involved again," said Bliss, getting up quickly to follow the woman out of the car onto the Thirty-fourth Street platform.

"Colin, it's Bliss," she said into a phone in a booth on the corner of Thirty-fifth Street and Ninth Avenue. "Maybe you don't want to talk to me. Maybe I don't want

120

to talk to you, but I have to. I don't know who else to call. I think I've found Nadine Knight."

"Where are you, Bliss?"

"She's gone into a hotel on West Thirty-fifth. I'm across the street in a booth on Ninth Avenue."

"Stay there, and I'll meet you," he said.

Ten minutes later on her Timex she saw him approaching the hotel. He saw her. He waved at the booth, but instead of meeting her he went into the hotel. Bliss waited. She began to perspire. Someone wanted to use the phone. She stepped out of the booth and waited in the doorway of the seedy hotel next door. She began to wonder if she really had seen Nadine Knight, or if her imagination had been so worked up by Louisa that she had invented her. Colin emerged from the hotel and crossed the street to where she stood.

"I checked the registry. There's an N. Olson listed. I called Mrs. Olson and Phil Knight. They're on their way."

"What do we do now?"

"We find a place to sit down — you look very shaky."

That was hardly the word for it. Bliss had begun to tremble as if she were a vibrator turned up to high.

He took her arm and gently led her toward Eighth Avenue. They passed a number of hotels similar to the one in which Nadine Knight had been hiding.

"Take deep breaths." Colin pushed open the door of a small coffeeshop. Most of the booths were empty. A few people sat dreaming over cold coffee. They slid into facing cracked plastic seats and looked at one another. "How did you know?" Colin asked.

"She was with Blackball when I first saw her. Subconsciously I must have known all along. That was why Louisa made me feel so guilty."

A waitress sauntered up to their table. "I'm very hun-

121

gry," Bliss said. "I want a hamburger and french fries and a chocolate soda." When the woman had gone, Bliss stared out the window. "You were right about me. I *was* rigid and judgmental. I was too scared not to be. I wanted my life to be safe and narrow. I wanted to Have a Normal Life and Be a Normal Person."

"Do you remember the lines, you must have heard them a hundred times, from *Private Lives?*"

"Something about how very few people are normal really."

"Deep down in their private lives."

"It all depends on a combination of circumstances."

She had heard Polly rehearse the words till she knew them by heart. "If all the various cosmic thingummys fuse at the same moment and the right spark is struck, there's no knowing what one mightn't do."

"That was very good," Colin applauded. "You might even end up closer to the stage than the very best seat in the house."

"How close is that?" Bliss wondered.

He reached across the table to take her hands, "This close?" he said, both answering and questioning her question

18

When Bliss got home, she heard Polly in the living room. There was someone with her. A voice called down the hall.

"Darlingest, you're home." It was Polly's mother, Ruth Prentice. She uncrossed her legs and reached up for a kiss. Crisp and cool in a tan pantsuit with a pink ruffled ascot frothing under her chin, her pretty face looked up like a flower. As she bent to kiss her Bliss breathed the scent of spice and mint that always surrounded her grandmother. Blackball curled contentedly at her side after a flurry of cheek licking and snuffling with the short sighs she resorted to when the pleasure of the moment was more than she could bear.

"I've been bringing Gran up to date," Polly said in the artificial TV sit-com voice she used with her mother. The hilarious Bliss and Polly show, a laugh a minute, was ON.

"Polly's been telling me all sorts of things. I've met this

heavenly dog, and heard the whole incredible story. Found on the subway, missing owner. After so much drama, even though I'm longing to hear more, I almost hesitate to ask what's new?"

"What's new? You want to know what's new?" Bliss began to giggle, the question struck her as so funny. She flopped on a chair facing the two women and leaned forward, her elbows on her knees.

"Tell us?" Ruth grinned, suspecting a funny anecdote.

"I found Nadine Olson Oaks Knight."

"You what?" Polly blinked theatrically several times.

"I found her on the subway, same as I did Blackball."

"How too divine. Do we feed her and walk her just like her dog?"

"I'm serious, Pol."

"So'm I. We can buy them matching coats and collars. If you get her a gorgeous doctor for her shots, maybe he'll marry *me*."

"Will someone explain what's going on?" Ruth said.

But before Bliss could draw breath, Polly began again. "She found the dog, why not the lady? Right, darling? I can take care of them both while you're at college. They'll be company for each other if not me."

"Please listen, Polly," Bliss said, trying to control her anger. "I saw her on the subway. She was the one who was with Blackball the day I found her."

"Ah, how our plot does thicken." Polly lit a cigarette with fanfare.

"And I called Colin." Bliss turned to her grandmother, attempting to ignore Polly's flippant interruptions.

"Colin? Who's Colin?" Ruth looked lost.

"He's a friend. He went into the hotel I trailed her to and found she'd registered."

"Under that unusual name, Missing Person. Any tags?" Polly blew a smoke ring.

"N. Olson."

"But darling, there must be heaps of N. Olsons. You never even met the lady. I mean I can certainly see why you'd have a pretty overwrought imagination on the subject, but this is such a big city." She turned to her mother, who looked as if she were trying to follow a conversation in a foreign language. "I am always telling Blissy to read less psychology and more romantic mystery and fiction. I think she's proving I made my point."

"I don't know why I never put it together before, when it was so obvious," Bliss began to speak in a rush. "I don't know why. She was with Blackball that first day. She said she didn't know anything about the dog except that it got on at Eighty-sixth Street. Then she threw Blackball a piece of bagel." Bliss closed her eyes to remember it better. "Of course that was so the dog would be distracted and not follow her out of the car. She left so fast. She was there and then she was gone. She had a couple of old shopping bags, a suspicious paranoid bag lady look. 'I never talk to strangers,' she told me. 'Don't get involved.' But she picked me out to take her little dog." Bliss opened her eyes wide with the wonder of it. "Blackball," she called to the dog, who immediately jumped from the sofa and onto Bliss's lap. "She selected ME. You both did." Bliss hugged the dog to her.

"It makes a marvelous story," Polly said, "but you don't have any actual proof that it was that Nadine Whatsername."

"Whoever the woman might be," Ruth interjected in her soothing professional voice, "Bliss had such wonderful, helpful motives."

Suddenly, to her own surprise and chagrin, it was all too much. "Oh stop it," Bliss burst out so loudly that both women jumped. "I'm not joking and I'm not fantasizing." But as she said the words her certainty took flight and she wondered at what had happened. Had her imagination run away with her? Had she, careful, plan-making, unspontaneous, down-to-earth Bliss, really gone too far? At this thought her voice and assurance gave way. Frustration and self-doubt overwhelmed her.

19

Just before she fell into an exhausted sleep Bliss heard Polly answer the telephone. "She'll call you in the morning, Jenny," Polly whispered.

In the morning she heard Polly's alarm go off, but the next time she awoke it was because Blackball had jumped onto her bed, and was noisily licking her paws. Strong light slanted through her window. All at once she knew that Polly had *not* awakened her, she would be late for school, and the telephone had been ringing for some time. She ran down the hall toward the kitchen. It was nine o'clock. Polly's note was propped by the salt shaker. Bliss grabbed for the phone.

"Darling." Polly was breathless. "It's all over the newspapers."

"What?"

"The whole story. I just picked two papers up at the newsstand. I'm coming home."

"What are you talking about?"

"Don't move. You can't handle this yourself." She hung up. Bliss stared at the dead receiver. Her stomach clenched like a fist. The sight of her mother's leftover coffee and crust of muffin nauseated her. The phone rang.

"I'm calling from the *New York Post*, Blissful; I wonder if I could talk to you for a minute."

She hung up. The phone rang again. It was Jenny. "This is incredible. Why didn't you tell me? It's all over school. Why aren't you here? Why do I have to read about you in the paper? Just because we haven't been on speaking terms for a few days you go and pull this on me?"

"What are you talking about?"

"You don't know? My God. Page one." She cleared her throat. " 'Missing actress, former wife of Lyman Oaks, found by the same student who found her dog.' Colin is quoted. Louisa is quoted. Louisa gave an interview. To top it all off Howard's run off with Sibyl."

"Is that in the paper too?"

"Listen to this. 'Like Mother Like Son.' That's the headline on the bottom. They left notes claiming that the pretense of a brother–sister relationship was wearing them down. They're at the end of the article. 'Mother Found, Son Lost,' it says."

"Who called the newspapers?"

"Francesca says that Lyman Oaks is a genius at publicity. This is fantastic free press for him. His name and the shows he produces are spread all over the *News* and the *Post*. Great big letters and pictures and everything." Jenny started to read again. " 'Ex-Wife of Broadway Producer Found after Four Months in Midtown Hotel.' "

"But how did Lyman Oaks find out?"

"Louisa called to tell Howard about your finding her mother. Howard was gone, so she told Lyman Oaks. Of course, the heroine of all this seems to be you."

"Me?" Bliss dropped like a stone onto one of the kitchen chairs.

Again Jenny began to read. " 'She found the dog, she found the Mother. Her name is Blissful Joy.' "

The operator cut in. "Five cents for the next five minutes."

"I don't have a nickel. By the way, are you still mad at me?"

"Mad at you? It was the other way around."

"To tell you the truth, I forget."

"I've got to go," Bliss whispered as the operator cut them off. She put her head on her arms on the table. Polly's key turned in the lock. She strode into the kitchen waving the morning papers over her head like triumphal flags. " 'Missing Actress Found by Student's Instincts.' "

The phone rang. "Are you psychic?" a high voice said. Bliss hung up.

"Pull yourself together, Blissy. A television news crew is coming over for an interview." Polly began to tidy the kitchen. "Colin called to tell me at the office."

"I can't."

"They're on their way. Colin's on his way too. He'll help you out. Now get dressed, for heaven's sake, and enjoy yourself. Who'd ever have thought it would be *you* who would get me a TV break."

"Oh Polly."

Polly looked sheepish. "And I'm sorry about last night."

Bliss brushed her teeth and got dressed. She heard Colin's voice. He was helping Polly remove stacks of papers from the living-room table. As she came into the room, the door buzzer went off and the babble and clatter of a TV crew setting up took over.

"Compose yourself," Polly hissed, like a stage mother.

"Where's the dog? Get the dog out here," a man said to Colin.

Blackball, suddenly shy, had slithered under the sofa and could only be lured out with a piece of bagel.

"Okay, get the girl on that chair with the dog in her lap," the same frenzied man directed. Then looking at Bliss for the first time, he smiled. "Hi, I'm Sal; sorry about the scramble, but this wasn't on my schedule today."

"It wasn't on mine either," Bliss said numbly.

"Right, okay. Just sit on that chair, relax, hold the dog. Let's get your voice register. Start talking. Tell us in your own way what happened."

The hot lights on her had a soothing, unreal effect. She saw herself as if she were outside her own body, watching herself on a TV set as part of the six o'clock news.

"I was sitting on the subway coming home from school," Bliss heard her distant, unreal, television embodiment say coolly, "when I saw this little black dog looking at me as if we were old friends. The woman next to me said, 'I can't tell you anything about it except it got on at Eighty-sixth Street.' She told me not to get involved."

"Did you want to get involved?"

"Oh no." The unreal Bliss smiled. "But I did anyway, and look what's happened." She began to count what had happened on her fingers, consciously playing to a TV audience. "I found a dog, the dog found my father his new wife-to-be. Louisa Knight found me. I found Louisa Knight her mother. It really is incredible."

"What do you think it means?"

"Means?"

"Do you think you've learned anything from the experience or could pass on any nuggets of wisdom you've gotten from it?"

"Like what?" Bliss shrugged.

"People should take risks, leave ruts, change safe ways of doing things, follow their feelings."

"Especially that one." Bliss was aware that he was trying to wrap up the segment.

Sal pressed a button on his recording machine. "Now would you nuzzle the dog."

Bliss nuzzled the dog.

"You realize you're a celebrity." The strong lights were turned off. The crew was packing up. "What will you do with it? TV anchor woman? Weather? Sports? My job? You just did a honey of an improv. A natural actress."

"An actress? An improv?"

The telephone was ringing again. The door buzzer was going off. Polly was flying from one to the other. Theater at last. Colin was leaving. Bliss followed him down the hall. "Where are you going?"

"Lyman Oaks, never a man to overlook the publicity value of an event, has asked me to audition for a part in his next production." As he opened the door a letter which had been wedged into the rim of the peephole fell to their feet.

"It's for you," Colin said handing her the letter addressed in the scratchy up-and-down script Bliss immediately recognized.

"It's from Sibyl." Bliss took Colin's hand. "Please wait." She opened the envelope and began to read out loud.

Dear Blissful,

We're sorry we did what we did. We hope you don't feel like a sap. Please don't be mad. We needed somebody and you were SHE. Howie and I met when our parents got married. I was twelve and he was fifteen. Young, but intense (remember Romeo and Juliet?). Mommy guessed, or intuited, or whatever it is stupid people do better than people who have more brains. Anyway she sent him away to boarding school and watched us like hawks when he was home. We learned how to trick her, but it's been getting worse and worse and harder and harder. One day I'll write my auto-biographical novel about it and Lyman Oaks will buy the stage rights and cast Brooke Shields's daughter as me. Anyway we thought it would be easier if Mrs. Oaks thought that I had introduced Howie to a friend and then Howie would actually "like" her. We picked you. It didn't work. We hated setting you up and then we blew it. We decided to cash in some bonds from birthdays and graduations and split. Howie's lined up a job and I'll look. We'll be out of the city and away from a situation that was driving us both nuts. Please don't hate us.

Sibyl

"Do you hate them?" Colin asked.

Bliss was so angry, hurt, and embarrassed it was hard to sort out her feelings at all. "They're crazy, running away like that. It's a neurotic crush. They've ruined their lives because of self-destructive, out-of-control emotions."

"I think you're contradicting some of the things you just said on TV." Colin turned a pinched profile to her.

"Sibyl and Howard 'went with their feelings.' You had some kind words to say for that."

"Sibyl and Howard went too far."

"I see," Colin said and hurried down the steps without saying good-bye.

Bliss wanted to call him back and ask him what he'd "seen," but he looked as if he had no intention of turning around.

20

Sal was right. When she returned to school the following day Bliss found she was a celebrity. She felt as if a halo surrounded her. Girls who had never bothered to look at her much less say hello came up to tell her they had seen her picture in the paper. The newspapers had described her as "pretty and bright"; "a model student."

"We better move to a long table," Jenny said at lunch; "otherwise I'll have to become your press agent. If they can't get statements from you they want bulletins from me."

"Did you use psychology to find Nadine Olson?" Susu asked.

"Psychology had nothing to do with it," Bliss said. "Nothing had anything to do with it."

"Where's Sib?" Francesca leaned forward on both elbows. "Have you got any clues? Are you going to find her too?"

"I'm through with finding people," Bliss laughed.

"But you must know something. She picked you out for a friend."

"Howard picked you out for his girl."

"They both picked me out for a patsy."

"The *News* says that Colin Bragg is your boy friend. Was he that dreamy-looking bartender?"

"I wish I could find a missing person," Jenny started to sulk.

Colin Bragg, boy friend. It was an established fact. Bliss's MRWMOS had been noted by the *Daily News* in a release fed them by the publicity office of Lyman Oaks Productions. "Talented young actor Colin Bragg, up for second male lead of *Crowns*, the new Lyman Oaks offering for fall, is the same Colin Bragg, boy friend of Blissful Joy Bowman, who helped identify both the dog and the ex-wife." When Bliss had read and reread these words, she had been afflicted by a combination of emotions, among them distress, delight, fear, and pride. She had no idea what Colin felt for her at this point or what he thought. She was dully aware of the fact that she thought of Colin a great deal. In the middle of class, concentrating on a problem written on the blackboard, she would realize that she had been thinking of Colin. A rush of embarrassment would overwhelm her. She was irrationally apprehensive about being detected in the act of Colin-dreaming. She looked forward to her first session at Mrs. McFee's to distract her from this new "mental spasm."

Mrs. McFee conducted her tutorial course for the SATs out of a small dark apartment in the West Fifties. She was a crisp plump woman with a glint of treason in her eye. "I'm the Benedict Arnold of Princeton," she said in a very brief introduction (she was already passing out the first practice test). "I know their tricks and I'll teach you a couple of your own. It's a game. You have to know how to play in order to do well. We've got less than two weeks, so let's get going."

When the thirty-minute test was completed she went over it with each student. There were four P.M. juniors and two boys from the Bodwin School. "Never take the questions in order. You'll waste precious time. Start with antonyms then move on to analogies and sentence completion. Save reading comprehension for last; they take the longest. Cluster them. You get better as you go along. Never read the paragraph. Read the questions first. If the question is about Washington, let your eye zip down the paragraph till you see Washington and read that sentence. What you know has very little to do with doing well on this test. Knowing how to take the test is what's important. We'll accomplish that by taking the test over and over and mastering the skills of test taking."

Bliss listened with growing amazement. The SATs had to do with innate aptitude as bridges have to do with window curtains. Nothing.

"In our next session I will teach you how to make good wild guesses," Mrs. McFee was saying in conclusion. "And of course we'll do more practice tests."

Bliss began to pack up her notes and books. Tricks and games. They trick you, you learn to trick them back. What if you were never a game player? If you didn't like tricks? Did that mean you were stupid? Unable to handle college work? NO. She answered her own question. The answer came with certainty from deep within herself. It came with an authority greater than she would find in any pamphlet or brochure hawking the validity of what she now knew was nothing more than a test which tested one's innate ability to take a similar test.

21

"It's been one week since I found Nadine Olson Knight," Bliss complained to Jenny, "and nothing's happening."

Jenny looked up from her chemistry notes. They had been quizzing each other at Jenny's kitchen table. "What are you talking about? You want drama like that every day?"

"I mean, Sib and Howard are still gone. Nadine Olson is in some hospital for her mental condition, and nobody cares. The newspapers have found something else to write about. I mean it's irresponsible."

"You mean you haven't heard from Colin," Jenny said.

Bliss shrugged. "He's busy rehearsing."

"Does he know how you feel about him?"

"Do *I* know how I feel about him?"

"If I were you I'd call him up and find out." Jenny dismissed the subject and went back to her notes.

"There's never any answer when I call," Bliss mut-

137

tered. "He's got one of those recording things that says, 'Leave your name and message, buzz beep.' "

"If it were me, I'd leave my name and message and go buzz beep."

Later when she was home gazing at the telephone and considering whether to take Jenny's advice, it startled her by ringing.

"Angel baby," Dan's voice sang into her ear. "We set the date. Circle the twenty-second of May and tell Black-ball she's the honored guest hound."

When she hung up, Bliss took out her calendar and circled the twenty-second in red magic marker. To make it stand out more than the ninth, she put petals on the circle. There would be life after the SATs.

"Remember," Bliss repeated on the morning of the ninth of May, as she walked with Jenny in a misty rain toward the doors of the Brandeis Junior High School where the test would be given, "there will be life after the SATs."

"You mean we are not about to die?"

Susu approached them from across the street. She held her two number two pencils, passport I.D., and ticket of entry in front of her like votive offerings. She looked even paler and more red-eyed than usual. "I have this fantasy," she said. "I dream about going that kid from Florida one better, and finding the test wrong on TEN questions."

"Since it's a fantasy," Jenny said, "why not find them wrong on everything?"

"They *are* wrong on everything." Bliss stopped walking to make her point. "They claim the results of this test judge innate aptitude. WRONG. They claim that doing well on this test means one will be able to handle college work. WRONG. They claim there's nothing you can do to prepare for the test. WRONG. Their own logic is so shaky that if you put their claims in a multiple-choice question, the answer would be 'None of the above.' "

"Wrong on three out of three; hey, I like that." Jenny smiled. "Maybe it gives us a chance to be right."

"And not to die," Bliss reminded her.

"Were we supposed to die?" Susu blinked and all three of them burst out laughing to the consternation and puzzlement of everyone around. They were still laughing as they took their seats.

One hour later, Bliss looked up from her booklet, caught Susu's eye, and winked. Susu winked back. Mc-Fee's had paid off. In the two weeks of tutoring, Bliss had raised her practice test score from four seventy on the first day to seven twenty on the last. She'd already zipped through the antonyms and analogies and begun the sentence completion. She was saving the reading comprehension for last, but knew she would have plenty of time. Taking control of the test in this way made her feel less like the victim she had been the first time she had taken it. Now she was arranging it and organizing it. Taking control. She wasn't quite enjoying herself, but she wasn't about to go under. As she finished the last question of the reading comps, she heard someone humming a tune from *The Pirates of Penzance*. At the very back of the room a familiar heart-shaped face was bent over a booklet. A familiar knobby hand was thrumming on a desk top. Sibyl Oaks, alive and well at the SATs. The bell rang.

As they filed out of their seats, Bliss saw a group begin to form around Sibyl. Jenny and Susu and Francesca were already at her side.

"I came down for these things," she was saying. "I had already registered, and I do want to go to college. Mummy's accepted our living in Burlington. I'll finish high school up there. Howie's going to the university next year. I hope to go the year after. It's still a little up in the air." When she saw Bliss she lowered her eyes and put out a timorous hand. Bliss took it and they shook.

"Thanks, Bliss," she murmured. "You did help me take some things seriously. It's changed my life."

"I have to thank you for helping me take some things *less* seriously," said Bliss. "It's changed *my* life."

"You mean this gibberish?"

Bliss nodded.

"Nobody's going to believe me, but I'm starved," Sibyl whooped. "Let's get out of here and find something to eat."

Relieved and ravenous, they headed toward the nearest pizzaria.

On the twenty-second of May, Bliss came home from school at three. First she washed and dried and combed Blackball. Then she twined a selection of artificial flowers around her collar. When she was satisfied with the effect — "a cross between a floozy and a diva" — she showered and dressed herself, slowly and carefully. She stood in front of the full-length mirror in Polly's room arranging her dress, a pale mauve cotton with tucked bodice and eyelit underskirt in which Polly said she looked like "one of those shepherdesses that's about to get kissed by a cherub." She was thinking of Colin, again. "Really, Colin," she tossed her head at the mirror, "I trust we can speak honestly. Would you care to define our relationship?"

It was time to go. She sprayed herself with Polly's

Chanel, leashed Blackball, and set off. The afternoon had turned soft and warm and full of the promise of summer. A brief rain had made trees in the square appear shiny, almost luminous, in new green foliage. Blackball, seeming to sense an occasion, began to parade, ears taut and nose up. Less than three months before, on a miserable March afternoon, Bliss recalled, they had walked to Dan's between banks of wet and melting snow. The snow had thawed. The trees were green. In the square, grass had pushed up in patches. They passed the corner where Blackball had first suddenly sniffed the air, and then run headlong, pulling Bliss behind her to the house with the red door. She had led Bliss to other places as well, to affection, to fear, to misrepresentation and painful truth. They passed the pet shop where Sibyl and Howard had played at pretending their feelings for her. She had been pretending too. She had invented feelings for Howard as if she were an outsider, a spectator of her own life, caring only for the "look" of it. Look at the nice young couple. So acceptable, such fine credentials. She had imposed the meaningless standards of strangers to her own life. She was better off trusting to her own standards. How could she learn them? Instinct and good sense.

A few doors down was the candy store where she had first been aware of Louisa Knight following her. Suddenly she was aware of someone else following her.

"Hello," said Colin.

Bliss stopped walking.

In a frenzy of greeting, Blackball dashed around their legs and tangled them both in her leash.

"Joined forever," Colin said uneasily.

"Don't panic." Bliss was more hurt than she would have believed. "I won't detain you."

"Oh don't rush off. I've missed you."

"Of course you have. I went around the world, you know, after . . ."

"Yes, yes, I know. How was it?"

"The world?"

"Yes."

"Oh, highly enjoyable."

"China must be very interesting."

"Very big, China."

"And Japan."

"Very small," Bliss said. "Like Manhattan. If you miss somebody all you have to do is pick up the telephone and dial. If you don't want to speak to them again, that's perfectly all right too. Of course you may bump into them on the street, which is embarrassing, but it's wrong to pretend you care if you don't."

Colin drew back. For a moment Bliss thought he might run for it. Instead he met her eyes levelly. "Caring for you was the problem."

"Problem?"

"You said so yourself. Sibyl and Howard. Neurotic, obsessive, self-destructive? You would have pinned me along with them in your last issue of *Psychology Today*."

"But I only said those things because I was so embarrassed and angry. Oh Colin . . ." She could not find the words to go on. Once again she had thrown up a wall of jargon to protect herself and once again she had been hurt by it. Blackball began to tug impatiently on the leash. "I have to go."

He looked at his watch. "So do I."

"Good-bye, then."

"Good-bye." But they continued to walk in the same direction. "I'm not following you," Colin said with the beginning of a smile. "I've been invited to a wedding. The bride is a lady vet I know and the groom is appearing in the same stock company as I this July. He wants me to meet his daughter. She was known as an impossible pain in the neck until about three months ago when she found a dog on the subway, tried to pass it off as her own, made several amusing miscalculations, met a fine young man, an actor who was guilty of a few miscalculations of his own, and has shaped up, this daughter, into a . . ."

"A fantastic young woman . . ."

"A fantastic young woman, exactly," Colin agreed, taking her arm as they entered Dan and Delphi's building.

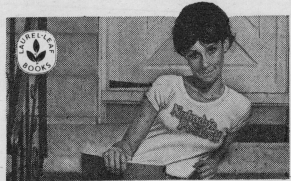

YOUNG Love
IS A VERY SPECIAL FEELING

Stories to touch your every emotion

_____ **CLOSE ENOUGH TO TOUCH** $2.25 (91282-2)

Matt Moran is engulfed in grief over the death of his first love—until he meets Margaret Chasen. She's older, and captivating. And by refusing to indulge his self-pity, she helps Matt learn about losing, taking chances, and beginning again.

_____ **DREAMLAND LAKE** $2.25 (92079-5)

When two boys discover a dead man in the woods behind Dreamland Lake, they're drawn into a mystery that ends in terrifying tragedy.

_____ **REPRESENTING SUPER DOLL** $1.95 (99733-X)

Indiana farm girl Verna Henderson longs for the bright lights and excitement of far off places. But when she becomes involved in the brittle, superficial world of a beauty contest, she comes to appreciate the solid values of her country life.

_____ **THROUGH A BRIEF DARKNESS** $2.25 (98809-8)

Sixteen-year-old Karen is whisked away suddenly from New York to England to stay with relatives she's never met. Her confusion and fear build as communication from home stops and she's left to piece together a mystery about her father that's haunted her for years.

LAUREL-LEAF BOOKS

The Austin Family Trilogy

MADELEINE L'ENGLE

____**MEET THE AUSTINS**   **$1.95 (95777-X)**
Orphaned Maggy Hamilton comes to live with the Austins
in the first book about their warm, fun-loving family.

____**THE MOON BY NIGHT**   **$2.25 (95776-1)**
The fun and foibles of the Austin family's cross-country
camping trip are described by fourteen-year-old Vicky
Austin—who is also struggling with the fun and foibles of
early adolescence.

____**A RING OF ENDLESS LIGHT**   **$2.95 (97323-9)**
Vicky, now fifteen, spends a difficult summer confronting
the problems of first love and the slow death of her
grandfather.

Laurel-Leaf Books

the Judy Blume Diary

The Place to Put Your Own Feelings

This diary is wonderfully different from most because it can be started on any day of any year. It's a <u>special place</u> to write about your own <u>special feelings</u>. Spiral-bound, THE JUDY BLUME DIARY features a letter from the author, quotations from her books, and 36 black-and-white photographs.

Like your thoughts, THE JUDY BLUME DIARY belongs to you. It's the place to put your own feelings, whenever and however you like.

YEARLING **$6.95**